me
&
jack

ALSO BY DANETTE HAWORTH

Violet Raines Almost Got Struck by Lightning
The Summer of Moonlight Secrets

me
&
jack

DANETTE HAWORTH

Walker & Company ✸ New York

First published in the United States of America in June 2011
by Walker Publishing Company, Inc., a division of Bloomsbury Publishing, Inc.
www.bloomsburykids.com

For information about permission to reproduce selections from this book, write to
Permissions, Walker BFYR, 175 Fifth Avenue, New York, New York 10010

Library of Congress Cataloging-in-Publication Data
Haworth, Danette.
Me & Jack / Danette Haworth.
p.   cm.
ISBN 978-0-8027-9453-6
Summary: During the Vietnam War, when twelve-year-old Josh and his
Air Force recruiter father move to a small town in the mountains of Pennsylvania
and get a dog from the local shelter, Josh is forced to stop hanging back and takes
on the unfriendly town residents, a mountain, and the meanest boy in school.
[1. Dogs—Fiction. 2. Bullies—Fiction. 3. Country life—Pennsylvania—Fiction.
4. Schools—Fiction. 5. Pennsylvania—History—20th century—Fiction.] I. Title.
PZ7.H31365Me 2011   [Fic]—dc22   2010034338

Book design by Danielle Delaney
Typeset by Westchester Book Composition
Printed in the U.S.A. by Quad/Graphics, Fairfield, Pennsylvania
2 4 6 8 10 9 7 5 3 1

All papers used by Bloomsbury Publishing, Inc., are natural, recyclable products
made from wood grown in well-managed forests. The manufacturing processes
conform to the environmental regulations of the country of origin.

For Chris

me

&

jack

chapter 1

I'd never been afraid of heights, but pressed against the passenger window looking over the side of the mountain, it seemed like a good time to start. Seat belts? Yeah, good idea. They would make it easier for the rescue team to find our bodies. I pulled mine tighter and braced one hand against the dashboard.

The station wagon chugged up the mountain like a roller coaster straining to make that first peak. A couple of times, the rear wheels spun out, shooting stone torpedoes. Dad clicked off the radio. I didn't argue; I'd seen the drop as we made that last hairpin turn. If he wanted to concentrate, I was all for it.

The car followed the snaky road back and forth up the mountain. On one side, we were nearly grazing the jagged wall of the mountain; on the other side, we were inches away from plummeting over the edge. Below, barns and fields of crops looked like a paint-by-number picture. Dad cranked the wheel hard at each turn. When he finally steered off *let's-defy-death* road, my foot released an imaginary brake and my back relaxed against the seat.

The road we were on now was well hidden by trees and the angle of its entrance. Every now and then we passed a cabin or an old trailer. On one property, a rock fireplace with a chimney sat in the grass. Vines latched onto it and climbed around its base. I could see where the foundation once was. It made me wonder what had happened to the house.

Finally, Dad turned up onto a side road and into a gravel driveway. Nothing but woods on both sides, except for the old house we'd parked in front of. Even then, the trees crept up to the house and stretched their knobby branches toward the roof like they were trying to touch it. The sun lit the treetops, but the woods below stood in darkness. A black forest.

I peered at the mountain through the windshield. "You think any wild animals live up there?"

"Probably just squirrels and birds." Dad took off his sunglasses. "Maybe bears."

"Bears!" I said, shooting a glance into the trees.

"Joshua, I'm kidding." He shook his head. "People wouldn't live here if it wasn't safe." He got out, opened the back of the car, and grabbed a couple of suitcases. "Come on, help me."

I struggled with a suitcase and followed him up the steps into our new home. The wood floor creaked and echoed our every footstep, and a draft blew at our backs. I shuddered right down to my feet.

When you move, you're homeless for a while. You don't live at the place you're leaving, and you don't live at the place you're going to. Sometimes you have to stay in a hotel for a couple of weeks, which is great because the hotel is full of other air force kids who don't care that they never met you before; they want someone to race with in the hallways or play catch with outside. But sooner or later, you have to leave and face your new life. Today's new life was in Cheslock, Pennsylvania, courtesy of my dad being an air force recruiter.

My room was upstairs, down the hall from Dad's. I ripped open a moving carton, pulled out my shoe boxes, and lined them up, one box of treasures for every place I could remember living. Six boxes so far, and that didn't include the new one for Pennsylvania. Lifting the lids, I eyed some of my stuff: my baseball trophy (best Little League team in Hickory, New Jersey), pieces of quartz (from a field in Tennessee), little bottles of sand (right off the dunes of Lake Michigan). I wondered what Pennsylvania would fill my box with. The only thing I really knew about Pennsylvania was one lame joke: *What's the biggest pencil in the world? Pencil-vania.* Yeah, I'd have them rolling in the aisles with that one.

I scanned my souvenirs one more time. My life, right here in these boxes. I pushed them under the bed and tore

3

open more cartons. They were full of stuff like clothes and sheets, and I went through them all until the last box had been emptied. You learn to do that when you're in the air force.

I looked at the flattened cartons, then out the window. I'd done enough. "I'm going outside," I shouted, running downstairs as I heard Dad yell the usual Dad stuff, "Be careful! Don't go too far!"

From the driveway, I spied on the house at the bottom of the road. No one in the yard. No hoop or bikes, either, so I was pretty sure I was the only kid around.

Crossing the side yard, I slipped past some bushes and into the woods. Oaks and maples towered over me, blocking the sky with their leaves. My skin felt cool and damp, and I picked up the scent of pine needles and blueberry bushes. Spongy green moss grew at the base of a tree. I brushed my fingers against it.

Then a flicker of movement caught my eye. I whirled around—bushes flashed their leaves, but I heard nothing and then everything was still.

"Hey!" I shouted. The woods absorbed my voice. My back prickled with chills. Suddenly the trees seemed too tall and the house too far, and I bolted through the woods until I reached our door.

Later, Dad and I sat on the porch and ate pizza off paper plates. Fireflies blinked across the yard. If Mom were here, she'd celebrate our first day in the new home by serving our pizza on china and our pop in wineglasses. She'd make up funny stories about people we'd meet and what would happen in our new town.

I sighed and pulled a pepperoni off my pizza.

"What are you going to do come Monday?" Dad asked.

I gulped down my lemonade. "What do you mean?" I took another bite of pizza, stretching the cheese till it broke.

"I'll be at work. You'll be alone all day."

I kept eating. I wanted to see what he was leading up to.

"I don't want you by yourself in the house. It's not like the base; there's no one here to watch out for you." He gazed past me into the woods. The trees looked even bigger now, black against the purple sunset. Dad shook his head. "I don't feel good about leaving you here alone."

I just about choked on my pizza. "Dad, I'm almost in seventh grade! I don't need a babysitter!"

"Not a babysitter." He turned, looked at me, and grinned. "A dog."

chapter 2

The next day, Dad and I entered the back of the dog pound, where all the cages sat. A single dog barked, sounding the alarm; then the other dogs joined in, barking and jumping, and it seemed they were all saying *Pick me! Pick me! I'm the best!* The barking made it feel exciting, like this was a happy place, but when I saw the rows of cages lined up and stacked, it looked like dog prison. I wished I could take them all home.

"What kind of dog did you have in mind?" The worker had to talk loudly to be heard over all that barking. He stuck his finger into a cage and scratched a little brown dog's ears.

"A watchdog," Dad said. "One to watch over the house and my boy while I'm at work."

"I've got just the dog for you. Picked him up yesterday."

We followed the guy down the row to a large cage. "German shepherd. About five years old. He'll do the job."

I looked at the German shepherd. He seemed all right, brown and black fur, dark brown eyes. He thrashed in his cage but kept his eyes on me, barking the whole time. His teeth looked sharp.

"I like him," Dad said. "What do you think, kiddo?"

I shrugged. "He's okay."

The pound worker told Dad more about German shepherds. I drifted down the row of cages and saw lots of mutts, a couple of poodles. I'd almost worked my way to the end when I spotted a dog standing at the back of his cage on the bottom row. I crouched to get a better look at him.

The dog stepped forward a bit and stopped. He didn't jump and bark like all the other dogs; he just held my gaze. His eyes were the color of caramel. A patch of white covered most of his chest, and a star appeared on his snout between his eyes. His ears stood straight up, like a rabbit's, and they were glowing red.

"Dad!" I yelled. "How about this one?"

Dad and the worker walked over. The dog backed up in his cage when they bent down to it.

Dad pointed at the dog's ears. "Kind of strange-looking, isn't he?"

I frowned. The dog rested his eyes on me openly, as if he knew me, as if he *trusted* me. Staring back, I felt the same way.

"I like him," I said.

Dad stared at the dog and nodded. "He does look very intelligent. What breed is he?"

"I don't know. Just found him in a fancy cage outside one morning." The worker straightened up. "He's been passed over a lot; most people say he doesn't seem friendly."

"He's friendly," I said. "He just likes to think about it." Same as I did.

"Today's his last day here, if you know what I mean." The worker looked at Dad.

Dad frowned and glanced toward the German shepherd. "I don't know. The other one seems a bit more—"

"This is the right dog," I said and stood up. "This one."

The ride home was short but took forever. The dog pushed against my arms, straining to stick not just his head but his whole body out the window. His nose twitched wildly and his skinny tail slapped my face.

When we got home, he darted from window to window, pressing his nose against the screens. I ran after him, but he ducked my every move like a basketball player. He pressed one screen so hard that it fell out and he coiled to spring after it, but Dad grabbed him.

"Shut that window!" he yelled. The dog squirmed in his arms, licking him and trying to escape at the same time.

I slammed the window shut and sat by Dad on the floor. "He likes you!" I said.

Dad smirked, pushing the dog off his lap. He wiped the slobber off his face. "I think this dog is going to be trouble."

The dog and I sat on the floor at the foot of my bed. One thin branch scratched at the window screen and the dog kept putting his paws on the sill to see what was going on. I was glad he was the kind of dog who liked to explore, because that's exactly what I liked to do. But first, he needed a name.

"What about 'Buddy'?" I asked. The dog did not lift his head. Buddy was not a good name. Not Rusty, either, or Lucky. "What about 'Rex'?" The dog huffed and gave a big sigh. I stroked his back. His fur was smooth like velvet when I rubbed it the right way, but it prickled like bristles when I rubbed it the wrong way. So far, I hadn't been able to come up with the right name for him. He was lean and strong, and that's the kind of name he needed.

I pulled a shoe box out from under my bed and showed it to him. "These are all my treasures from New Jersey." The dog snuffled into the box. A piece of paper stuck to his nose. I laughed and pulled off the paper. It was Scott's address, my best friend from New Jersey. He was the fastest runner in school. Reaching into the box, I grabbed a baseball. "This is from my Little League team. Everyone signed it." The dog inspected each signature and licked the ball like he knew we had been a good team.

I put the baseball back into the box. The best box I'd saved for last. Mom's locket was on top, a long chain with a big heart on the end of it. When you pop the heart open, there's a picture of me and Mom. She's holding me tight and laughing with her head thrown back.

"This is my mom." I held the heart open to where the dog could see it. Everyone always said I got my hazel eyes from her. I got my brown hair from Dad.

The dog looked at the locket and then looked at me. His eyes looked sad.

"She died when I was in fourth grade." My eyes got that achy feeling, but I held them open to make it go away.

The dog licked my cheek and pressed into me, laying his head and chest on my lap. That almost broke me, him nuzzling me like that. I put the necklace down and scratched his ears.

I dug through the box and found a cardboard coaster from when Mom and Dad first met. On the front it said "Jack Daniel's Old Time Tennessee Whiskey." Written in lipstick on the back was Mom's phone number from when she still lived with her mom and dad.

"See that?" I showed the dog. He lifted his gaze to the coaster and then looked at me like he wanted to hear more. "They met at a dance," I began. "When he asked for her phone number, she didn't have a pen. So she used her lipstick." I looked at him and he pawed the coaster.

"Jack Daniel," I said. When the dog heard that, he popped his head up and stood. We looked eye-to-eye at each other. "Jack Daniel," I repeated. Jack barked. I got up and jumped onto the bed. "Jack! Jack!"

Jack jumped around the bed barking and I jumped up and down whooping until we heard Dad holler, "Stop it! You sound like a bunch of wild banshees!"

I leaped off the bed. "C'mon, Jack! Let's go outside!"

We burst out of my room and raced downstairs to the back of the house, passing Dad in the living room. "Later! Me and Jack are going out!"

"Whoa, whoa, whoa!" Dad shouted. Piles of paper covered the coffee table. The scrapbook Mom had started for Dad was on top; every time he made the newspaper, Mom would clip the article or photo and tape it into the scrapbook. Dad stood and stretched his back. "Jack, huh? Is that what you named him?"

I nodded. "He likes it."

Dad clicked his tongue. "C'mere, boy."

Jack's whip of a tail wagged as he loped over to Dad. Dad tousled Jack's ears. "You know, I've missed having a dog around. I always had a dog growing up." His face gladdened as he roughhoused with Jack. "I like his name," he said. "It suits him." He glanced over the stacks on the table. "I'm going to need more coffee if I'm ever going to finish going through all these papers."

Jack and I followed him into the kitchen. I pulled my shoes on. I never untie them; I just pull them on or push them off with my other foot.

"Put that collar on him, and the leash," Dad said. "And stay out of trouble!"

"I will!" I said and barreled out the door with Jack close at my heels.

chapter 3

We ducked into the garage and I rolled out my bike. The hill we lived on was so steep I had to brake all the way down. Jack jogged easily at my side; he didn't seem to mind the leash at all. At the bottom of the hill, we turned right. I picked up speed and Jack ran faster, too. He looked like a racehorse. I pedaled as fast as I could, and he matched me.

We coasted around the bend, and I saw a couple of boys playing basketball in a driveway. I took a deep breath and slowed down as we got closer to them. My first new people. Having done this a million times, I knew how to make my approach—say hi; don't act too eager; play it cool—but I still always got that nervous feeling in the pit of my stomach. One kid had wavy, light blond hair, and he dribbled the ball toward me. The other kid was average in every way—not fat, not skinny, a little taller than me but not like a giant or anything. He acted like I wasn't there. I did notice he had kind of a big butt.

"Hi," the blond kid said.

I gave him the head jerk, that quick kind of nod that means hello. I don't like to act too friendly at first, because you can't take any of it back if the other kid doesn't like you. Still, he did walk over to me and that was a good sign. I squeezed my brakes and put my foot down. Jack stopped, too, standing at attention by my side. The mailbox read "Miller."

The blond kid dribbled the ball in place a few times, then said, "I like your dog."

"Thanks. His name's Jack," I said. Jack huffed a little when he heard his name. "I got him at the pound."

The other kid shifted on his feet. "Come on, Ray." He wiped his forehead with his arm. I saw he wore a leather wristband. Pretty cool. But he didn't even glance at me, so I didn't say anything to him.

Ray knelt down to pet Jack, but Jack backed away from him. "It's okay, boy," Ray said, holding out his hand for Jack to smell. Jack backed against my leg and looked at me.

"He just has to get used to things," I said. I leaned over and petted Jack so he wouldn't feel all alone.

The screen door wrenched open. A little girl leaned out and yelled, "Alan, Mom's coming—oh! *Doggie*!"

New kid rule: always listen. The other kid's name was

Alan, and he must be the little girl's brother. I filed that information in my head.

She skipped down the porch and right up to Jack. Jack didn't even move away.

"Wow," I said.

Still squatting, Ray said, "He likes you, CeeCee."

It was true. Jack nudged his head into her hand, all the better for petting.

"I like him, too," CeeCee said. She tipped her face up to me. "Are you his dog?"

"No," I said, feeling the corner of my mouth lift into a grin. "I'm his human."

Alan clucked his tongue. "Get away from him, CeeCee!"

I couldn't tell if he was talking about me or Jack.

CeeCee acted as if she hadn't heard him. "Hi, doggie!" She patted his head and scratched his ears.

"I said get *away* from that dog!" Alan said. "Plus, I thought you said Mom was coming."

CeeCee stood and twisted her face at him. "You're not the boss of me."

"It's okay, Alan," Ray said and stood up. "This dog's okay." Then to me, "Is he a show dog?"

Before I could answer, Alan sighed loudly and dragged himself closer, but he stopped short of joining us. "Why does he have red around his eyes?" he asked, curling up the corner of his mouth. "Is he sick or something? He looks weird."

My eyes narrowed. "He's not weird."

He raised his chin at me. "Well, he looks weird. What kind of dog is he?"

"A good dog," I said, gripping my handlebars tightly.

The kid sneered, then shouted, "His nose is turning pink! Oh man! What a weird dog—you should've named him Rudolph." He shook his head. "Wonder why the pound didn't kill him." Then he snatched the ball from Ray and ran down the driveway. "C'mon, Ray!" He shot the ball through the hoop. "Yeah! Two points! Later, kid!"

I wanted to shout—I don't know what I wanted to shout—but my mouth and my brain got stuck.

"Come on, CeeCee!" he yelled. "That dog might bite you."

CeeCee stared at her brother with her lip stuck out. Then she turned to me, her eyes big and blue. In a soft little voice, she asked, "He won't bite me . . . right?"

I bent down to face her. "Of course not! He's a nice dog. Plus, he likes you."

She looked up at me and smiled. "What's your name?"

"Joshua."

"I'm CeeCee."

Ray stood. "I'm Ray. Your dog's cool."

"Thanks." I tried to look friendly, but I had a hard time concentrating on it. "Who's that kid?"

"Do you know Prater Lumber?" Ray asked. When I shook my head, he said, "Well, he's Alan Prater." Ray made it sound important; I added a mental note to my file.

I watched as Ray pulled a yo-yo from his pocket, throwing it down hard, then flicking it up to wind the string around his fingers in a web. It should have knotted, but then he slapped his hand and the yo-yo spun down and back up into his hand.

"Nice." I'd only seen that kind of stuff on TV.

Ray grinned and spun the yo-yo absentmindedly while he talked. "I'm working on a combo for the July Fourth festival. Hopefully, I'll have enough saved up for the Groove-it by then."

"What's that?"

He caught the yo-yo around his back. "It's a better yo-yo for string tricks."

Closer to the garage, Alan bounced the basketball from side to side. "Ray! Put the stupid yo-yo down and let's play already."

An expression passed over Ray's face so quickly, I almost missed it—he pressed his lips together and rolled his eyes. I glanced toward the hoop, where Alan Prater made easy baskets from the side. Probably thought he was a big shot. If I called him Alan, he'd think we were friends or something. I'd call him Prater.

Ray slipped the yo-yo into his pocket.

"So he doesn't live here?" I asked.

"He's my brother," CeeCee said. "He's twelve and I'm five. I'll be in kindergarten next year. Alan's scared of dogs." She fished in the pocket of her shorts. "Do you like candy?"

Whoa, scared of dogs. I fixed my eyes on Prater. "Yeah . . ."

"Want one?" She held out a butterscotch to me. It looked kind of grubby, and lint stuck to the parts that weren't wrapped, but I took it anyway. Every new kid knows that rule: never say no to friendliness.

She popped one into her mouth and started talking about Missy, her best friend who she saw every day, and they liked to play dolls, except Missy has the most important one, which is the Ken doll, and everyone knows the girl doll needs a boyfriend, but CeeCee doesn't have one and—

Prater's afraid of dogs. I wanted to get back to that but didn't know how.

"Come on!" Prater shouted from the hoop.

We watched as Prater threw the ball but missed. Guess he wasn't as good as he thought he was. He looked up and caught me staring. "Take a picture, why don't you?"

I would, but it would probably break the camera. That's what I wanted to say. Instead, I stood there like an idiot.

Ray asked, "You want to play?"

Yeah, but not with Prater around. Sometimes you have to break your own rules. I shook my head. I wasn't saying no to friendliness—I was saying no to Prater. "I have to take Jack for a walk."

I couldn't wait to get away from there. Jack and I rode back the same way we came. Prater the pear. Prater the crater. Prater the hater. Ray was okay, but Prater was a jerk.

I pedaled furiously. Jack galloped at my side. My heart pounded and I gulped huge lungfuls of air, but the pace was nothing to Jack. His powerful strides easily matched my pedaling. His ears and nose looked red, like someone blushing, and his skinny tail curved stiffly over his back.

When we got to our road, I struggled to pedal straight up, but the hill was too much. I got off the bike and pushed it.

Wonder why the pound didn't kill him.

I decided I hated Prater. Worse, I hated that I froze and didn't stick up better for Jack.

That night, I lay on the bed with Jack curled next to me. I was supposed to be asleep, but we were both restless. A cool breeze drifted in from my windows, and Jack kept lifting his snout to it, sniffing and nodding. That's how dogs collect information.

If humans could get information that way, being a new kid would be so much easier. You'd smell people before you even saw them, and the smell would tell you everything you needed to know. Some people's smell would say, *I am an idiot.* You'd tell yourself, *I don't want to meet that kid*, and then you could just avoid him. You wouldn't have to worry about what you should have said or what you should have done.

Jack shuffled around on the bed, moving closer to the edge. Then he jumped off and rested his muzzle on the window. Kneeling beside him, I gazed beyond our driveway to the woods. A wall of darkness. Dark, but not quiet. A breeze rustled the treetops and it sounded like the ocean. Crickets chirped. I even heard a bird.

I don't know what Jack could see, but his nose twitched like crazy. He was a good boy. I'd be prepared for Prater next time. No one was going to cut my dog down.

chapter 4

I figured God would forgive us one Sunday, but Dad didn't see it that way. I put on a scratchy church shirt and some pants, and we were off. The pastor stood at the door of the church, greeting everyone who strolled in. I saw Ray, almost shouted, but then I saw Prater walking ahead of him. I pretended to be looking at something in the opposite direction.

"Newcomers!" the pastor said as we reached the vestibule. He shook our hands and asked Dad where we were from. Dad said New Jersey. When people ask me where I'm from, I say the air force, because we never stay in one place long enough to be from it. Turns out the pastor had once served as a navy chaplain.

"At least you're working for the same boss," Dad joked.

The pastor chuckled, then looked serious. "How's it going? Seems like a hard time to be a recruiter."

That was an odd statement. The government was drafting guys right out of high school to fight in Vietnam. It sounded like a *great* time to be a recruiter—you didn't even have to find guys to join the air force; the government found them for you.

"It doesn't make me popular," Dad said. "But I've got only two years till retirement."

"Got any plans?" the pastor asked

"I'm thinking about college," Dad said. "I'll be thirty-eight when I retire, probably the oldest freshman on campus, but I'm thinking about it."

I fidgeted through most of the service, picturing Jack at home waiting for me. The only time my ears pricked was when the pastor mentioned a local boy in Vietnam. "We have good news from the Zimmermans." He gestured toward them. Heads turned and, looking in that direction, I saw a man put his arm around his wife. She smiled, lips quivering, and wiped her eyes with a tissue at the same time. "Their son Mark is scheduled to come home in July."

Clapping and people yelling "Thank God!" filled the sanctuary. Mrs. Zimmerman nodded tearfully to the people around her.

After it died down, the pastor spoke again. "We have much to be thankful for. But I also have some bad news." He paused. "Even though they don't go to church here, most of us know the Kowalski family." Murmurs buzzed around the pews. The pastor looked over us, took a breath, and laid his hands on

22

the podium. "Their son David has been reported missing in action."

A gasp went up. Dad straightened in his seat. I snapped to attention. Missing in action—MIA. That could mean he'd been taken prisoner or had been injured or killed but not found.

"This is a boy we all know. He went to high school with our kids. This family—this mother and father—they are our neighbors." The pastor gripped the sides of the podium. "This isn't about politics. This isn't about your views on the war. This is about a family we know and love." He let out a deep sigh. "Let's pray."

I bowed my head. I'd seen pictures of the war in magazines. Vietnam didn't look like anywhere I'd been before. It had strange trees and rice paddies and huts. In some photographs, soldiers crouched in grass so tall, all you could see were the tops of their helmets. I saw one photograph of a soldier carrying another guy in his arms. The photo wasn't in color, so all the blood was black. There was a lot of black in that picture. I didn't like to think about it.

When we finally got home, I raced Jack upstairs and changed into shorts and a T-shirt. "Dad!" I yelled, bounding downstairs. "We're going for a ride!"

I almost knocked Dad down in the kitchen.

"What about lunch?" he asked.

Jack danced around by the back door. "He needs to go outside," I said.

Dad leaned down to pet Jack, but Jack jumped around so much he nearly bashed Dad in the face. "He's wild!"

I felt pretty wild myself. After almost two hours in church, I needed to move around some. We'd go past Ray's, see if he was outside. I started out the door, but Dad stopped me.

"Don't forget this." He lifted the leash off the hook and tossed it to me.

Frowning, I caught the leash, then Jack and I burst outside.

Dad didn't know Jack like I did. He didn't know how fast Jack could run or how Jack stuck to me like glue. Glancing over my shoulder, I saw that Dad wasn't looking through the window; I jammed the leash into my back pocket.

If Ray wasn't out, we'd keep going and see what else there was that way. There might be other kids farther down or on a side road. It was worth checking out; you don't know which friends are going to work out or not, so it's good to not count on any one person.

I backed my bike out of the garage. Jack trotted ahead, danced in front of our house, and stopped. His ears turned toward the woods, antennae picking something up. Then he bolted across the side yard.

"Jack!" I threw my bike to the ground. "Jack!"

He slipped into the trees. I tore after him. He leaped over a branch and disappeared. I ran through the woods, following the sound of leaves and twigs snapping ahead of me.

The trees grew denser and the angle sharper. Prickers caught my legs, and I tripped over a log, but I kept climbing up. All I could hear was my own breathing and footsteps. Trees towered over me. My lungs burned and my heart felt like it would burst. I stopped. It looked the same everywhere. Nothing but trees and silence.

He was lost.

I lost him.

The leash was still in my back pocket. "Jack!" I shouted. "Jack!"

A single bark cut through the air. I tramped on the undergrowth, climbing over a steep bank. There stood Jack in a small clearing, his head held high, his chest out, and his legs planted in a stance that looked like he was ready for anything.

I collapsed to my knees, bracing my arms against my thighs. Sweat trickled down my back. My hands and legs were dirty, and blood was smeared on my legs.

Jack trotted over. He licked my face and sniffed around me, tail wagging the whole time. His ears blushed. I pulled him close and hugged him. "Jack, don't ever run away like that again." I looked into his eyes. "What were you chasing?" He licked me again. I could hear his heart beat clean and hard as I pressed into him.

I pulled the leash from my pocket. I hesitated for a moment, then snapped it on.

A birch tree stood beside us, its bark hanging off in ripples. I carefully peeled a thin layer; it was crisp and held the curve of the trunk. I wanted to write on it like they did in the old days.

Suddenly Jack lunged at the end of the leash, his nose twitching, his ears erect. Then I heard it—a chuffing sound. Fear prickled my scalp. Jack strained against the leash.

"No, Jack." My voice came out as a whisper.

I heard it again, then silence. My heart hammered against my chest. I scanned the clearing. Nothing. Tugging on Jack's leash, I said, "C'mon, Jack, let's go."

We sprinted down the mountain, cutting past blueberry bushes, dogwoods, and maples. I remembered the general direction, but Jack seemed to remember every inch we had covered. We came out of the woods at the same spot we entered. My bike lay on the driveway.

A door slammed and Dad stepped out onto the porch. A deep line formed between his eyebrows.

Jack and I raced across the side yard to the porch. "Dad, Dad, there's a bear up there!"

His eyebrows drew closer together as he jogged down the porch steps. "What?"

"Up in the mountain. Jack chased it!"

"You saw a bear up there?"

"Yeah! We heard it!"

"Wait a second." Dad shook his head as if to clear it. "You *saw* a bear, or you *heard* one?"

"We heard it, and Jack chased it all the way to the top of the mountain."

He cocked one eyebrow. "You went up the mountain? Alone?"

"I wasn't alone—Jack was with me." I stopped. I could see he was deciding if I was in trouble or not.

He looked at my legs and frowned. "You've been bleeding."

"Prickers."

He crouched and brushed his fingers against my legs. "The bear didn't do this?"

"No, I told you . . ."

A little smile played around his mouth. He stood up, leaned against the porch, and crossed his arms. Case closed.

"*Dad!*"

"What?" Dad shrugged and put on an innocent face.

I crossed my own arms. "You don't believe me."

Dad laid his arm across my shoulders and led me onto the porch with Jack. "Listen, kiddo, I believe you heard something, but it could have been anything." He held open the front door, and Jack and I walked through. "You're letting your imagination get the best of you. Now get washed up for lunch."

I frowned and looked away. He was wrong. Something was up there, I was sure of it. Something silent with watchful eyes.

chapter 5

pparently, I wasn't safe enough with Jack. Dad hired a lady to come in. "Just a couple of times a week," he said. "Besides, aren't you tired of pizza?"

Millie slipped Jack a treat the first time she came over. That alone made me like her, but when she said his eyes were wise and knowing, that clinched it for me.

Today we were taking Jack to the vet's. I couldn't wait to find out what kind of dog he was. Going through our encyclopedias, I found all kinds of special breeds, but I didn't see one dog that looked like Jack. He had to be something extra special.

"Something rare," I said to Jack, roughing him up a little before I put the books away.

While we waited for Millie, I remembered the birch bark and went upstairs. The bark still held the curve of the tree trunk when I lifted it from my Pennsylvania shoe box. I grabbed a pencil and, using a book as a table, began to write on the inside of it. The pencil lead poked through the bark, so I ended up writing on real paper and sticking the bark in the envelope.

Dear Scott,

Pennsylvania is boring. I met one kid and one jerk. But the good news is I have a dog now. His name is Jack and he's a fast runner. Maybe you can visit and meet him.

I got this birch bark off a tree on the mountain I live on. I will try to get some more later.

Your friend,
Joshua

We walked out to the mailbox just as Millie pulled into the driveway.

"You ready?" she called out.

"Yep." I swung open the door and Jack leaped in, scrabbling his front paws along the dash. He pranced on Millie's lap, turned his backside to her, and nearly whopped her with his tail.

"Hi, Jack!" Millie said, leaning to avoid getting hit. "One happy dog."

I laughed. "Sure is." I realized how lucky we were to get a lady who was not only nice, but who was a dog person as well.

Sitting on top of an exam table wasn't one of Jack's favorite things to do. He pedaled his legs and barked, trying to escape. The assistant told Millie and me to hold Jack down while she got the doctor.

"What do we have here?" Dr. Hart asked when he came in. That didn't sound like the kind of question you actually answer, so I didn't say anything. He walked around the table without taking his eyes off Jack. "Very unusual dog. Is he . . . what is he?"

"They didn't know at the pound," I said, straining to keep Jack still. "I was hoping you'd know."

Dr. Hart looked thoughtful. He leaned in and cupped Jack's head. "Hmm." He spread Jack's eyes open, then looked at his teeth. "Hmm."

"What do you think?" Millie asked.

Dr. Hart crinkled his eyebrows. "I don't know." He scratched the back of Jack's ear. "Good musculature." He turned to me and smiled. "Bet he's fast."

"He's really fast."

He looked at Jack. "He resembles a greyhound, but his ears aren't right, neither is his coloring. See the way his ears and the rims of his eyes are turning red? I've never seen that trait before."

"Is he sick?" Millie asked.

"No!" Dr. Hart laughed. "You've got yourself a healthy, well-cared-for dog here. Alert, intelligent. About a year old, I'd say. But that blushing—that's unique." He put the stethoscope up to Jack's chest. "I'll be darned if I know what kind of dog he is."

On the way out of Dr. Hart's office, I saw a flyer for something called the American Dog Breeders Association. Picking it up, I read that the ADBA was a dog club for purebreds and their owners. It also said that dogs were good for people and that dogs had rights. I slipped the flyer into my pocket. Maybe they would know what kind of dog Jack was.

That night, Dad pulled out the roast that Millie had put in the oven before she left. Her cooking was almost as good as Mom's and definitely better than Dad's. Jack lay at my feet under the table, and when Dad wasn't looking, I slipped him a few chunks of meat. He thought it was good, too.

After supper, I made Dad get out Mom's Polaroid camera. That's a camera that makes pictures right when you take them. He snapped one of Jack all alone and then one of me and Jack together. The pictures rolled out of the camera and Dad was careful to hold them by the edges as he laid them on the table. At first, the picture is nothing except all black. But that's a trick the camera people have figured out. I stared at the black pictures and slowly, the black faded, colors seeped in, and before I knew it, I was looking at pictures of Jack and me.

"Unique." Dr. Hart had used that word for Jack. Also "unusual" and "distinctive." And not just his ears or his nose or his lips. "I've never seen dogs with eyes this color," he'd said. "Amber." The dictionary said amber was a dark orange-yellow, or a see-through yellowish-brownish color. To me, his eyes looked like jewels or tigereye marbles.

Before I went to bed, I wrote a letter to the American Dog Breeders Association and put Jack's picture in the envelope. I leaned the picture of me and Jack against the lamp on my bedside table. Jack was already stretched out on the bed. There was just enough room for me.

chapter 6

My arm felt sore the next morning from where Jack had laid his head most of the night. Dad smiled at me when I came into the kitchen. He was already having breakfast—cereal and orange juice.

When I sat at the table, I stretched my arms wide and accidentally knocked over the cereal box. Cheerios scattered onto the floor. Jack licked them up instantly. I looked at Dad and we both laughed.

When Dad asked me to get the paper for him, I stumbled over Jack on my way to the back door. The newspaper lay on the driveway by the garage. I opened the door, but before I could go out, Jack squeezed past my legs. He rushed down the steps and tore around the house.

"Jack! Jack!" I turned back into the kitchen. "Dad!"

Dad was already out of his chair. "What? Did he take off?"

I started to run, but Dad grabbed me and stepped onto the back porch. Putting two fingers in his mouth, he delivered an earsplitting whistle.

"Dad!" I tried to push around him. "That's not going to do it—we have to go get him!"

Another whistle, straight into my ear.

I pushed through and ran down the steps.

"Hey!" he yelled. "Put your shoes on."

"Dad!"

He gave me the look.

It would be faster to listen to him than to argue, so I jumped on the porch and slid my feet into my sneakers. I rushed down the steps and around the house. I didn't see Jack anywhere. I faced the woods and held still . . . no telltale snap of leaves or branches.

Dad jogged up behind me, holding the leash in one hand. "Where did he go?"

"I don't know." If he didn't go up, he must have gone down.

I started down the hill, not waiting for Dad. If he'd let me run after Jack immediately like I'd wanted to, we'd already know where Jack was. Now he was nowhere in sight.

Dad caught up to me as we reached the bottom of the street. Before, Jack and I had turned right, but I didn't see him that way now. I looked left. The left side had more houses and they were on both sides of the street. My heart sank. He could be anywhere.

"Right or left?" Dad asked.

"I think we—"

Just then I heard a commotion down the street to the left. Jack bounded out from behind someone's house. A lady followed after him banging two pot lids together.

"Jack!" I yelled. Dad whistled. Jack caught sight of us and ran toward me. His gait was easy, and his ears glowed. He planted his big front paws against my chest and then he jumped and danced around me. I ruffled his ears. "Jack! What were you doing?"

Dad handed me the leash. As I snapped it onto Jack's collar, Dad turned.

"Uh-oh," he murmured.

Generally speaking, the words "uh-oh" are never followed by anything good. I stood up and looked at Dad. He stared in the direction the lady was coming. Then I saw his features rearrange into his air force face—the way he makes his face look when he's in full dress uniform. I stood a little straighter and tried to look like he did.

"Did you see what your dog did?" the lady yelled. Her head bobbed as she marched toward us. Her face was all pinched together. Each hand clutched a pot lid, as if she'd bang them like cymbals if we didn't answer properly. "Did you see what he did?"

"No, I'm sorry," Dad said in a deep voice. "The dog was too fast for us this morning." He stepped forward and offered his hand. "I'm Rich Reed. This is my son, Joshua."

She put one lid under her arm and shook his hand. Then she smoothed her hair. It seemed like for a second she forgot what she was mad at. "Well, it's nice to meet you. I'm Sylvia Puchalski." She took a breath. "I'm sorry to tell you this, but look at what your dog did." She pointed down the street. I didn't see anything, just houses. And overturned garbage cans.

"Jack didn't do that!" I said.

She didn't even look at me, just kept her eyes on Dad. "Mine's knocked down, too," she said, "and I caught him running through my flowers." She pointed back to her yard. "And I don't mind telling you that I came right out after him. He was tearing up my irises and I—"

As if to prove her point, Jack jumped and pranced around my legs.

"I can see from here you have a beautiful garden, Sylvia," Dad said in his rich voice.

"Well, thank you, I . . . thank you."

Dad turned to me. "We'll take care of any damage the dog caused, right, Joshua?"

My jaw dropped. "But, Dad, Jack didn't—"

"Joshua!"

I almost rolled my eyes but caught myself. I looked down and scuffed my foot against the road. "I'm sorry about your flowers and your garbage cans."

"We're both sorry," Dad said. "And I'll have Joshua clean up the mess."

I jerked my head up. That wasn't fair. But I didn't say anything.

Mrs. Puchalski seemed happy now. She told Dad she hoped he liked it here. She said she knew how hard it was to get started in a new place and if we needed anything to give her a call. She'd be the last person I'd call.

When she started back to her house, Dad waited a few seconds before heading toward ours. Jack leaped over the leash, tangling it around his legs. I bent down and unwrapped it. "Why do I have to clean up that lady's garbage?"

He let out a long sigh. "Because Jack knocked it down."

"How do you know? She didn't see him do it."

"Joshua, he came flying out of there." His voice was low, like he didn't want anyone to hear. "Just pick up her garbage can and all the other ones he knocked down."

I stopped. "What? That's not fair. Jack didn't do anything."

"But he might have. Listen"—Dad glanced upward—"not everyone's happy to have an air force recruiter next door. We have to work extra hard to show them we're good neighbors, and that includes Jack."

"Why wouldn't they want us as neighbors?" And what did the air force have to do with it?

We started walking again. "It's not really us." He rubbed the back of his neck. "It's just . . . a lot of boys have died in this war. A lot of people don't think we should be over there."

I remembered that local boy the pastor mentioned.

"Do *you* think we should be over there?"

Dad started to say something but closed his mouth and shook his head. "I don't know," he finally said. "But *we're here*, and we have to be extra-good neighbors. It's just the way things are, nothing personal."

It sounded kind of personal to me.

"Don't forget about the trash cans."

Yeah, I got it. Basically, I had to pick them up so people wouldn't be mad at us because Dad was a recruiter. That stunk. And it wasn't fair, either.

"C'mon, Jack," I said. We ran ahead, all the way to the corner and partway up the hill before I needed to catch my breath. Dogs had rights, too, like the pamphlet had said. Besides, it didn't make sense—Jack couldn't have knocked down all those trash cans in such a short time, and plus I didn't hear any noise.

When we got into the house, I unhooked Jack, kicked off my shoes, and we shot upstairs to my room. After a few minutes, the stairs creaked with Dad's footsteps, and I heard the sounds of him getting ready.

Letting out a big breath, I sat beside Jack and looked directly at him. "You didn't knock down those trash cans, did you?" He did not look away and now I was sure of it—he was innocent. "I believe you," I said.

I caught up to Dad in the kitchen. He had his blues on; that meant he was going out on a recruiting call today. When I was little, Dad seemed like a different man in his uniform, the same way Clark Kent does when he's Superman—like a hero. Even now the sight of Dad in his dress blues filled me with pride. Made me want to be strong like a hero, too. "Dad, Jack didn't—"

"Stop." He closed his eyes for a moment and shook his head. "Just make it right."

I couldn't believe he was making me do this.

"Joshua, I'm talking to you."

I cocked my head. "Yes, sir."

He sighed and his shoulders sagged. Dark circles ringed his eyes. "Look, I've got to go to work. I want you to pick up all that garbage and leave Jack here when you do it, okay?" He paused for a moment. I said nothing. "Okay, I'll be home at five thirty." He stepped closer and ruffled my hair.

I watched him walk all the way to the station wagon, his head down.

I turned to Jack. "What a crummy day." I sat on the floor and pulled on my shoes. "Listen, I have to leave you here so I can go pick up all that stupid garbage."

Jack pushed his nose into my face, leaving a wet streak on my cheek. I laughed. "You're a good boy." I patted the top of his head and slipped out the door.

The garbage was slimy and gross. Coffee grounds, broken egg shells with slimy egg stuff, *diapers.* The trash cans smelled like spoiled-rotten food and poop. My stomach lurched.

I had only a few more to do when I spotted a couple of kids coming my way on bikes. I bent my head down. Let them keep going. Suddenly, gravel crunched and flew through the air. I spun around.

Prater!

He'd almost skidded right into me. I straightened up, angry.

"Ha! Scared you!" He wore a dumpy blue shirt and that stupid wristband.

I wiped my hands on the back of my shorts. "No, you didn't."

"Yeah, I did." He snorted. "You jumped."

Ray rode up beside us and stopped. His eyebrows pushed together as he looked around. "What are you doing?"

My face flushed. I was standing in a circle of wadded-up diapers. "I—"

"What do you think he's doing?" Prater said. "He's looking for something to eat."

The heat deepened in my face. I looked from Prater to Ray. "My dad said I have to pick these up." I waved toward the other trash cans.

"Why?" Ray asked.

Shaking my head, I rolled my eyes at the unfairness of it all. "Some lady said that Jack knocked these over, but he—"

"Who's Jack?" Prater interrupted. "Don't tell me you've got a brother."

Ray leaned forward on his bike. "Jack's his dog, remember?"

"Oh, yeah—Rudolph," Prater said, jerking his head back. "Where is your stupid dog, anyway?"

"I don't have a stupid dog."

"Well, then, I guess you're stupid because you're the one who's picking up all this junk." Before I could even think of a response, he turned to Ray. "Come on, Ray, let's go."

"Hang on," Ray said, then turned to me. "What are you doing after? You want to come with us?"

Prater stepped between Ray and me. "He can't. My mom already made plans for us." He looked at me. "See you around, kid." He rode off slowly. Then, like Ray was his own personal property, "C'mon, Ray."

Ray glanced at him, and turned back to me. "I guess I better be going," he said.

"Yeah."

He lifted his foot to the pedal and turned his handlebars. "We're going to shoot targets tonight. Want to come?"

Dad had a big thing against guns; he believed in fighting for our country, but he didn't believe in killing for sport. Neither did I. "What kind of targets?"

"Like paper targets. Alan's dad lets us shoot in their back-yard, but only after he's home from work. You want to come?"

"I don't know." I'd never held a gun before. Sighing, I glanced Prater's way. He was now halfway down the block, circling lazily in the street. I didn't want to be anywhere he was, but I did want to be friends with Ray. I'd already turned down two invitations: playing basketball when I first met them, and hanging out now because of this trash. If I turned down another invitation, it might be the last. "Where does he live?"

"Not far. Where do you live?"

I pointed to my street. "Up there. The only house on top of the hill." Prater began to ride back to us. "You better go," I said, gesturing my head toward Prater.

Ray turned and shouted, "I'm coming!" Then to me, "I'll come by after supper and get you."

Prater closed in on his bike. I started picking up the garbage; I wanted Ray to leave before Prater made his way back and opened his big, fat mouth. "See you later."

"See ya." Ray pushed off.

Okay, I had just made plans to engage the enemy on his own turf. As I bent to the next trash can, I watched Ray and Prater pedal down a couple of blocks and around the curve. Finishing quickly, I ran home. I couldn't wait to wash my hands.

chapter 7

ost people hide keys under a pot or the doormat. These are not good hiding spots because everyone knows that everyone else puts keys there. I put mine in the thumb of a dirty garden glove that I left by the back door. After I got into the house, I locked the door right behind me like my dad said because you don't want any robbers or murderers sneaking in.

Jack almost knocked me over when I came in. He didn't like staying alone in the house. I got us a snack, some cookies for me and bologna slices for Jack, and took them on paper plates to the den. By the time I got the TV on and flipped through a few channels, Jack had gobbled down his whole snack.

Gilligan's Island was on. Gilligan must have done something wrong because Skipper just hit him with his hat. I settled onto the couch. I used to watch this show in New Jersey. It was good to see Gilligan and Skipper again.

If I were stranded on the island with them, I would never worry about getting back to the mainland. Skipper was like a dad, the professor was like a smart uncle, Mr. and Mrs. Howell could be your rich grandparents, and Mary Ann and Ginger were pretty. Everything you need, right there on the island.

Jack and I sat on the couch even after *Gilligan* was over. A show came on where people jumped up and down and tried to guess the price of things. I thought about going over to Prater's tonight. I wished I could bring Jack; that way, at least someone who liked me would be there. But since Prater's dad would be with us, Prater wouldn't be able to act like a jerk. Then he'd see I was an okay kid. Plus, his sister was nice and so was Ray. I nodded to myself—maybe it would work out.

Sighing, I petted Jack. He harrumphed and settled even closer to me. His body was warm. I stared at the TV without really watching, just hearing the bells ding on the show.

The phone ringing woke me up. I sprinted to the kitchen.

A man's voice blasted through the earpiece. "Is this the recruiter's house? Richard Reed?"

"He's busy." That's my standard answer when I'm home alone. "Can I take a message?"

"Yeah, I've got a message for him. You tell him to stop

calling my son. Tell him if he stops by here again, I'll run him down the driveway with a baseball bat. You got that?"

Loud and clear. I hoped he didn't know where we lived. I tried to keep my voice from shaking as I asked for his name.

"Fritz Davies. You make sure he gets my message."

"Yes—"

He slammed the phone down.

I felt like he'd be pounding at the back door any second. Clicking off, I checked the locks and dialed Dad's office.

"Fritz Davies?" he said after I told him what happened. "Son of a— Listen, sit tight. Don't worry. I'm calling him right now."

I gripped the phone with both hands. "Why's he so mad at you?"

Dad sighed. "He's trying to get his son Steven to go to college, but Steven doesn't have the grades. He's got buddies going over. He wants to go with them."

I knew right then that Steven would soon be reciting the Oath of Enlistment. Being a soldier made you part of a brotherhood, just like being an air force kid. It didn't matter whether or not Steven believed in the war—he believed in his friends, and that would be his strength.

Dad spent a few minutes reassuring me that he'd take care of Fritz Davies, then we hung up.

Jack's spot on the couch was empty. I looked all over for him before finding him by the back door.

"Want to go for a walk?" I asked.

He jumped up and down and turned in tight little circles. I hooked on his leash, locked up the house, and we left. We jogged into the woods at the same place Jack had slipped in the other day.

A light breeze lifted the branches, and they swayed back into place. Sunlight flickered through the trees. Walking from shade to shafts of sunlight, I felt cool and warm at the same time. The trees right near the house had skinnier trunks than those a little higher on the mountain.

I spotted some blueberry bushes. A hint of red still colored most of the berries. I picked a few and popped them into my mouth. Juicy, but a little sour.

"Want one?" I asked Jack. I pulled off a berry and fed it to him. He sat there for a second, then he opened his mouth and let it roll off his tongue. Then he sneezed. I laughed and petted him. "Okay, you don't like blueberries."

I picked up a flat rock and began to dig a hole. If you dug a hole deep enough, you'd tunnel straight through to China. My friend Nick and I tried to do that until our moms came out and yelled at us for messing up the flower bed. That was when I lived in Missouri.

Jack helped me dig. His paws furrowed so fast that the hole quickly became deeper. Bugs and a worm crawled in the dirt, and then I spotted a couple of strange rocks.

"Jack! Stop!"

I reached into the hole and pulled out the rocks. They were flat and smooth and shaped almost perfectly like triangles.

I whisked the dirt off with my fingers. These weren't just regular rocks.

"Arrowheads! Jack, look!" I held them flat on my palm. The last person who touched these was an Indian, a real Indian. Closing my fist over them, I couldn't believe how lucky I was. An Indian had touched these and now I was touching them.

I looked at the arrowheads for a long time. I imagined a strong brave running silently through the woods. Spotting a deer, he drew back his bow and the arrow flung through the air. Or maybe he used these arrows to fight against soldiers or another tribe. It didn't matter—these were definite treasures in every way. An excellent find for my Pennsylvania shoe box.

I slipped them into my pocket and suddenly felt hungry enough to eat a horse. "C'mon, Jack," I said, giving the leash a light tug. We trotted through the woods all the way to the back door. I picked up the dirty garden glove, shook the key into my hand, and Jack and I ducked into the empty house.

chapter 8

I sat on the bank across from the garage with Jack on one side of me and a pile of rocks on the other. I'd discovered the chalky ones burst if you threw them hard enough. "Okay," I said, picking up one that was lemon-shaped, "here goes an M26." Pretending to ignite a grenade, I hurled the rock against the garage roof and watched it explode into a million pieces. They rolled down the shingles, dropping from the garage like hail.

My arm was cocked for another attack when I heard the station wagon revving up the hill. Finally. I wanted to show Dad the arrowheads but more important, I had to talk to him about going over to Prater's.

While our TV dinners were in the oven, I parked myself beside Dad on the couch. He lowered the newspaper. I held open my palm. "Look what I found today."

He leaned over, picked one up, and stared at it. "Let me see the other one." When I gave it to him, he looked at them so hard, I thought he was X-raying them. Then he turned to me with an amazed expression. "These are arrowheads!"

"That's what *I* thought!" So far, so good. It wasn't like I was going to lie to Dad about anything, but I knew I was warming up for the big question. When I was younger, other boys shot at each other with cap guns, but not me. I wasn't even allowed to own a squirt gun.

"Guns are not toys," he'd always say whenever I begged for one.

"Yes, they are," I'd whine. Mom and I passed them in the grocery store, for crying out loud. I'd tug on her hand, plead, and still she'd shake her head. *Your dad said no.*

I wondered what he'd say tonight. I wondered all through my mashed potatoes and sick-looking peas. The steak was as hard to chew as leather, so I moved on to my apple turnover compartment.

"Nothing like a gourmet dinner," Dad said. He'd eaten two of them. "I've got a few phone calls to make, okay?" He pushed back his chair.

"Wait." I swallowed and looked at the steak. I'd give it to Jack later. "Um, you know those boys I met? The ones playing basketball the other day?"

He smiled, ready for good news.

"Well, I saw them today and they invited me to come over after supper."

"That's great!" He relaxed in his chair. "I'm glad you're making friends. What are you guys going to do?"

I took a deep breath and exhaled. "They want to shoot targets. Prater's dad will be there," I added quickly.

Dad frowned.

"His dad will be there," I said again.

Staring at his folded hands, Dad mulled it over, then stood. "What's his name again?" I told him, and he went straight to the phone book. He called a few Praters before landing on the right one. After introducing himself, he made some small talk with Mr. Prater, then started asking questions. "What kind of guns? What kind of targets? How much experience do the other boys have?" I cringed in my chair. "Where will they be shooting?" Okay, I was officially overprotected. I just hoped Prater didn't get wind of this or I'd have to listen to more of his wisecracks.

I cleared the table while Dad said good-bye. Pretending to be busy by sliding our chairs back into place, I waited for his answer. Dad grabbed the dishrag, soaped it up, and wiped down the counter.

"Look at me." Dad turned from the sink. White soap bubbles glistened on his hands, but there was no mistaking that a US serviceman stood before me.

I straightened my posture and gave him my full attention. "You can go."

"I can? All right!" I headed for the back door, but Dad caught me by the arm.

"Listen," he said, his eyes dead serious, "I'm letting you go because I trust you." He lowered his chin before going on. "A gun is a weapon; I want you to respect that. No playing around, okay?"

"Yessir," I said. He'd fought in the Korean War. This was a big deal for both of us.

"Okay," he said and gave me a sharp nod—*dismissed*.

Jack and I waited for Ray on the front porch steps. I wondered what it would be like to shoot a gun. Soldiers fired guns all the time, but their lives depended on it. Plus, they trained with guns. I'd never held a gun before, much less shot one. The main thing was to not mess up in front of Prater. No way did I want to give him another thing to rag on me about.

Suddenly, Jack stood erect, and he focused on the bottom of the hill. Ray came pedaling up the road. I waved. This is how it starts, a friendship.

He cut over to his right, like he was going into Mr. and Mrs. Nichols's driveway. I almost shouted to correct him, but then he turned and cut over to the opposite side. He zigzagged all the way up the hill; it was ingenious—he never had to get off his bike.

"Hi, Ray!" I jumped down the porch steps to meet him.

"Hiya." Ray's face was pink from the ride. He laid down his bike and looked around. "Hey, I was right," he said. "I knew your woods and Alan's woods were connected."

"Really?" Great—Prater was my neighbor.

"Yeah, if you cut through your woods that way"—he pointed to the right—"you'll end up by his yard. I mean, it's like a few blocks over; the woods are really big."

"Oh." As long as I didn't have to see that jerk from my backyard.

"Where's Jack? I thought I saw him," Ray asked.

Jack had been right at my side on the steps; I leaped onto the porch and found him around the corner. He seemed relieved when he saw me. I bent down and stroked his head. "C'mon, Jack, it's all right." I tried to lead him out, but he balked. He looked up at me like he wanted me to stay.

"It's all right, Jack, he's nice." I rubbed his back. "C'mon, boy," I said. "Come on."

Jack rose slowly and walked with his tail drooping. He followed me down the steps but stopped just short of being near Ray. He held his head straight. It wasn't like he was afraid of Ray; it was more like he was being careful. "He just has to get to know you," I said.

Without moving closer, Ray crouched and held his hand out—not stretching his arm all the way, just holding it out a little. "C'mere, Jack." He waited. When Jack didn't come, Ray moved a little closer and touched Jack's head, scratching him lightly behind the ear.

I could see Ray was a dog person. I could also see that although Jack allowed Ray to pet him, Jack was actually inspecting Ray to see if he was a good person or not.

Ray must have passed the test because Jack relaxed; he looked like he was enjoying the petting.

When I put Jack in the house, Dad looked up from some paperwork near the phone. "You be careful."

"I will." Jack pushed behind my knee, almost making me fall. Dad kept his eyes on me. "Don't worry," I said, but I knew it was useless. Dad looked like he wanted to hug me. I pushed open the screen door and yelled good-bye.

"Have fun," I heard him shout as I lifted the garage door for my bike. "But be careful!"

I winced at his loud caution, hoping Ray didn't hear him. After I closed up the garage, I hopped on my bike and sped out of there, hollering to Ray as I neared the porch. *Please don't let Dad come bursting out the front yelling more warnings.* He'd hammered Mr. Prater with all those questions, and plus it was just target shooting. Nothing to worry about. Ray joined me as I turned down the hill.

Nothing to worry about at all.

chapter 9

Ray and I braked all the way down the hill and turned left at the bottom. We rode for a couple of blocks, passing Mrs. Puchalski's house. I followed Ray when he turned left onto a hard dirt road lined with trees. The road curved around and opened up to a huge brick two-story house that looked like a mansion. The yard was fancy, with rosebushes and a water fountain with a statue in it. The lawn rolled up toward the woods and even they were cleared of underbrush, like a park.

I heard the whinny of horses and saw a barn that was bigger than my whole house. A couple of horses and a pony trotted within a corral. I'd never been this close to horses before. The two big ones were a deep chocolate brown, and their manes were almost black.

Prater was rich.

"Man," I said. My eyes widened.

"Yeah, I know," Ray said.

We cut over to a small path that circled the corral. A breeze mingled the sweet, grassy smell of hay and the scent of horses. Prater came out from the barn, hooked a rope onto the pony, and led it to the fence by us.

Up close, the pony's coat shone. His mane was darker than his coat, and it was combed over to one side. Even though he wasn't as big as a horse yet, his legs were well muscled and he walked proudly.

"Hi," Prater said. He looked at Ray.

"All done?" Ray asked.

"Yeah, let me just comb him down and rub his legs." Then he turned his weasel eyes on me and said, "Didn't bring your dog, did you?"

This wasn't starting out well. I tried to think of something good to say, something funny or cool, but all I came up with was "Nice pony."

"He's not a pony, dummy," Prater spat. "He's a foal. Don't you know anything?"

The muscles in my face tightened.

"Come on, Alan," Ray said, shaking his head. "You knew what he meant." Then he turned to me. "Most people call baby horses ponies, but they're really called foals." He smirked at Alan and then looked at me. "Don't ever make horse mistakes in front of Alan."

Prater laughed.

I nodded. Anyway, who cares? I was just trying to be nice.

Prater rubbed the foal's nose. His eyes filled with pride. He reminded me of myself with Jack. "You're looking at a future champion," he said.

Without meaning to, I nodded my head in agreement. The foal was beautiful, so dark its coat almost shone blue. No white spots anywhere.

When I looked up, I caught Prater watching me. He tilted his head toward me. "You ever touch a horse before?"

I shook my head. Prater pulled the foal closer and stroked the side of its neck. "Like this," he said. "Not too close to his eyes."

I brushed my hand down the horse's hard and muscular neck. His mouth quivered and he ground his jaws, revealing big square teeth. I snatched my hand back.

My eyes darted toward Prater, but he didn't laugh. "He's just chewing against the bit."

"What's his name?" I said.

"Shadow." Prater patted the horse's neck. The look he gave the horse was gentle. Maybe he did have a heart.

"Look at this." He thrust his left arm to me, the one sporting the leather wristband. Holding the band so the etching was on top, he tapped it lightly. "See? It's Shadow. I made it with my leather kit."

I took a close look. Though it could have been any horse,

Prater made him look majestic, his front legs raised in a buck, mane flying in the wind. I liked it. "Pretty cool."

"Thanks." Prater looked back to Ray. "Let me put Shadow up. You guys can go on back if you want. I'll be right there."

Okay, that went all right. If the rest of my time at Prater's passed this easily, I could handle it.

Ray leaned his bike against the fence, so I did the same. We headed up the lawn, toward the woods. A few large trees stood here and there, separating the barn area from the rest of the yard. One tree had uprooted and fallen over; its base was taller than my dad.

"Is this still his yard?" I asked.

"Yeah, the yard even goes into the woods." He pointed to the left. "That's where I think if you cut through and kept going, you'd end up in your woods. They own a hundred acres." The yo-yo came out and he started flipping it around.

I leaned against a huge oak tree. The trunk split into a Y about fifteen feet up and boards had been nailed across the thick limbs, forming a floor. A couple of guns lay in the grass at the foot of the tree. Prater was still in the barn. Maybe we'd never even get to the guns.

"So, are you guys best friends?" I asked.

"He's my cousin." Ray sat down. "Well, not my cousin exactly, but my mom and his mom are cousins, so I guess we are, too." The yo-yo whirred around Ray's fingers. "Eiffel

Tower," he said, gesturing with his hands. He'd woven the string into an exact outline.

"Wow."

"If you want, I can show you how to do some of this stuff," he said. "Alan thinks it's stupid."

That's probably because he can't do it, I thought, but I didn't say that. What I really wanted to know was why Prater was scared of dogs. I leaned forward, the question forming in my mouth—

"Joshua! Joshua!" A pink flash darted out the back door of the house and up the hill to where we sat. Breathless, CeeCee collapsed in front of us. "Guess what?" Her eyes were full of a secret, a not-too-secret secret, because it was obvious she wanted to tell.

I played along. "What?"

She squinched her eyes and tipped her face up at me, big smile. Very big smile.

"You lost a tooth!"

Pleased with my answer, she tucked her legs under and leaned over to me. "I'll get a dollar tonight!" she said. She opened her palm to reveal a tiny tooth. "See!" She stood up and danced a little jig. "The tooth fairy's coming!"

Part of her dance involved fluffing Ray's hair around. He lifted an eyebrow, then tried to grab her without looking. She dodged his arm and kept fluffing and singing.

"Go on, Cee-monster," Ray said. "Quit bothering me."

She laughed and paraded around the oak.

Then Prater trudged up the hill holding the paper targets. I had hoped it would get too dark before he finished with Shadow, but it looked like there was no way out of it now.

"You guys ready?" he asked.

"Ready! Aim! FIRE!" CeeCee hollered, leaning out from behind the oak.

"CeeCee," Prater said. Same gentle voice he used with the foal.

She pursed her lips. Her arms folded and snapped against her chest.

Shaking his head, Prater laid the targets on the ground and led CeeCee away from the oak and toward the house. "You know you can't stay when we're shooting targets."

She whirled out from under his hand. "No fair! Daddy lets you play with guns."

This had the sound of an ongoing argument.

Sure enough, Prater sighed. "I'm older than you are. Besides, the guns are too heavy. You could shoot your own foot, and the kick might knock you down."

Her face puckered. "I might knock *you* down!"

She ran over and kicked his shin. I stifled a laugh—she looked so tiny against her brother. He easily captured her, turned her toward the house, and pretended to yell. "D-a-d . . . CeeCee's trying to shoot guns with us!"

"No, I'm not!" She squirmed in his arms. "Let me go!"

He let her go, then raised his eyebrows. "Then get back to the house or I *will* tell."

"Anyway," Ray said, "it's hot out here. I wonder if someone could make us some lemonade."

She stared at him to see if she was being played. Then she glanced at all three of us and broke into a big smile. "I'll make it for Joshua! Mommy will help me!" She ran down the hill and disappeared into the house.

Ray smirked at me. "Someone's got a crush on you."

My face heated up.

"Shut up," Prater said. He grabbed the targets. "Let's see if we can hurt these things."

Interesting choice of words.

I glanced toward the house and barn, but I didn't see his father anywhere. Prater was making his way up the lawn, getting ready for the big shootout. Lagging behind, listening to Prater talk with Ray about stuff I didn't know, I got the feeling I wasn't even there, or maybe I just didn't *want* to be there. Where in the heck was Mr. Prater? "I thought your dad was going to be here."

"He is." Prater shrugged. "He's in the house."

Great. Now Prater could act any way he wanted. Plus, Dad only let me come because he thought Mr. Prater would be here with us. But it would be all right; Ray and Prater had done this lots of times. Nothing bad would happen.

Ray stood at the bottom of the tree and looked up. The yo-yo was out of sight. "Man, this tree house is going to be great."

Prater walked up beside Ray. "Yeah, wait till it's done." Then he glanced at me. "Did Ray tell you about it?"

When I shrugged, he went on. "It's going to be like a little house. And on this side"—he motioned with his hand—"there'll be a window but with no glass. Dad's planning to mount a pulley with a line for targets." He pointed to the fallen tree. "It'll be hooked up to that tree. Then I can sit in the tree house and practice shooting from a stand."

Ray nodded. He knew what Prater was talking about. I'd ask Ray later.

Prater walked past us and nailed a poster onto the overturned tree. A bunch of black circles inside of each other and a bull's-eye right in the middle. I sighed.

Ray dropped a block of wood on the grass. "This is where you stand."

Prater grabbed one of the rifles, loaded it, and stepped up to the block. He cocked the gun, brought it to his eye, and fired. It was loud, but not as loud as I thought it would be.

"Ha!" Prater said. "Look at that." A hole showed through one of the rings of the target.

"Good one!" Ray said.

Ray took a turn, hitting the white part of the paper outside the target.

"Pretty good," Prater said.

It was my turn. My hands felt shaky as I took the rifle from Ray. The barrel was warm. The gun was long but not too heavy. I tried to shoot like they had, but the rifle just snapped.

Prater laughed through his nose. "You have to load it first."

I glanced at him and then at the rifle. I scanned the barrel trying to remember exactly how they had done it.

He snorted and grabbed the gun from me. He took a shiny brass bullet from a box beside the block. "Like this," he said. He pulled the lever down, and the casing from the used bullet popped out. Then he dropped the new bullet into the same compartment and snapped the lever closed. "You can carry the gun around like this 'cause it can't shoot. Then if you see something—" He spun toward the target, pulled the hammer back, and fired. Another neat hole inside the target.

He held the gun out to me. "Try again."

I gave him a sharp nod and took the rifle from him. The barrel was even warmer. Bending down, I took a bullet from the box and stood up. Prater's tiny eyes watched everything I did. The lever was easy to pull down, but the casing popped out and startled me. I almost dropped the rifle. Prater huffed. I slammed the lever shut.

"Hey, be careful!" Prater said. "That gun used to be my dad's."

I acted like I didn't hear him.

The hammer was hard to pull back. I had to use both thumbs. Slowly, I raised the gun and tried to steady it, but I couldn't hold it perfectly still.

"Come on, already," Prater said.

My eyes darted to him and quickly back to the target. I took a deep breath, let it out slowly, and squeezed the trigger. I expected to feel the power of the gun, maybe even be knocked back a little, but it was just kind of a loud *pop*. A wisp of smoke trailed out of the end of the barrel.

"Good try," Ray said.

"Yeah, right," Prater said.

There were still only three holes in the target. "Did I hit it?"

"No!" Prater grabbed the rifle. "Just watch me." He loaded, cocked, and fired. *Blam!* It tore a fourth hole into the target, this one even closer to the bull's-eye. He turned to me, smug. "That's how you do it."

Ray took a turn, hitting an inside ring, and then it was my turn. I was determined not to mess up again in front of Prater. I couldn't care less if I hit the target or not, but Prater cared—this had become a test I had to pass in order to be friends. I popped out the casing, loaded the bullet, and tried to pull the hammer back with one thumb like they did, but it was too hard. Again, I had to grip the rifle with two hands and use both thumbs to cock it. This time when I raised the gun, I steadied it against my shoulder, squinted, aimed, and squeezed the trigger.

Prater clicked his tongue in disgust. Still five holes. Heat seeped into my face.

He grabbed the rifle from me and exchanged it with the

other gun. "Here," he said, thrusting the new gun at me. "Maybe you can use this one. It's a BB gun. BB for babies."

"Geez," Ray said.

"What?" Prater asked. "Just joking."

I pushed the BB gun back to him. "Naw, I think I'm done shooting. I'll just watch."

"Okay, little baby."

"Alan," Ray chided.

Prater rolled his eyes. He raised the BB gun and fired toward the target. A neat little circle appeared near the bull's-eye. "Ha!" he shouted victoriously. He sent Ray to the barn to get another BB gun, and then he asked, "Hey, kid, ever go hunting?"

I looked at him. This was some sort of trap, something he would make fun of me for. "Why?"

"Just wanted to know." Prater lifted the BB gun up and got ready to fire. I turned an eye toward the target.

Pop. He cranked the gun again, aiming up a tree to the right of the target. *Pop. Pop.* What was he doing? I looked through the branches. A squirrel clung to the branch, staring at Prater.

I didn't even think about it—I pushed him just as he got off the next shot.

He whipped around and glared at me. "You idiot! What'd you do that for?"

Prater was bigger than me, and I could see up his nose. I forced myself to stare back. Out of the corner of my eye,

I saw the squirrel dart into the next tree. "You could've killed him," I said.

"I *would've* if it hadn't been for you. What are you," he snarled, "a wuss?"

"No!" I tried to stand my ground. "It's just—you don't need to be shooting innocent squirrels." The moment I said it, I wished I hadn't. I mean, I believed what I said, but it didn't sound very he-man, especially since Prater thought he was some big gunslinger.

He drilled holes into me with his eyes.

When I didn't say anything, he gathered the bullets and the other gun, then yelled to Ray, who was coming back, "Forget it! He's a wussy!"

It was one thing to have Prater call me that—he was an idiot—but if Ray laughed at me, I was done for. That would be it for me and him as friends.

Prater told him how I knocked off the shot.

Ray looked from Prater to me, then up in the branches. "I like squirrels," he said.

Prater huffed. "Whatever. Let's do something else."

"Lemonade!" CeeCee hollered from the back porch.

I followed them down the yard, not quite behind them, not quite with them either.

On the bike ride home, I told Ray about the arrowheads Jack and I had found. He stopped by to see them. "Wow," he said, inspecting the arrowheads under the light in my room. He pressed his thumbs against the points. "These are cool. Maybe we could find one for me."

"Sure," I said. Jack had draped himself across my legs, and I petted him. "How about tomorrow?" When Ray hesitated, I added, "I mean, if you're not busy with Prater or anything." I shrugged to show it didn't matter to me either way.

He handed the arrowheads back. "Well, I *am* supposed to go over to his house tomorrow. Could Alan come?"

My next words came out before I even had time to make them up. "My dad says I'm only allowed to have one friend over at a time when he's gone."

Ray nodded. Good, he believed it. I pushed the shoe boxes back under the bed. "So, does Prater always shoot squirrels?"

Ray sighed. "He shot a deer once, but his dad had to shoot it again because it was still alive. They like to go hunting."

It figured—Prater and his dad, out shooting innocent animals. I said, "Does everyone around here hunt?"

"Not really. I know I don't like to." He frowned. "Once, when I was little, I went over to Alan's house to play but no one answered the front door, so we went around to the back and this huge deer was hanging upside down from the roof of the porch. It was all bloody and ripped apart where the bullet had come out."

I made a face. I would never hurt an animal on purpose.

"Alan was, like, all excited because his dad was going to give the antlers to him," he said. "The deer was kind of

66

twirling, and when its face turned, it was looking right at me. Uncle Bruce told me it was Rudolph. I started crying—I mean, I was only five. My mom yelled at him for saying that, and then my aunt had us go in the house."

I imagined the deer, strung up like meat at a butcher's, its eyes staring. *Rudolph.* "So your uncle was there, too?" I asked.

He looked confused for a second, then said, "Uncle Bruce is Alan's dad. We've always called each other's parents 'aunt' and 'uncle.' "

One big, happy family. "So do all of you ride horses?"

"Yeah, you ever ride?"

"No, I've never been on a horse before." I didn't feel stupid admitting that to Ray. "Do you ride a lot? At Prater's house?"

"I ride some," Ray said with a shrug, "but not too much. His dad doesn't like to break their training by having other people ride them. He's even pickier than Alan."

I kind of liked hearing him say something bad about Prater. "Yeah, he's picky," I said.

Ray tilted his head and looked at me sideways. "What do you mean?"

"I mean, you know, like what you just said." I tried to sound casual.

He raked his fingers back and forth through the carpet. "He's picky, but he's okay."

I did not want to hear that. "But why did he try to shoot that squirrel?"

Ray shrugged his shoulders. "I guess he's used to it, you know."

I wasn't willing to forgive Prater that easily. "He didn't even care if he killed it."

"I know," Ray said, then he looked directly at me. "But he's my cousin."

chapter 10

Jack and I spent the next few days going down roads we hadn't been on before. A few kids were outside, but we didn't really meet anyone. That was okay; I had Jack. Some days, I didn't even ride my bike; I'd just run with him.

We got home from one of our runs to find Millie at the kitchen table with a plate in front of her and another plate in front of an empty chair.

"There you are!" she said. "I was getting ready to eat without you."

I laughed and sat down. Jack settled at my feet. Millie sure knew how to fix lunch: a ham and cheese sandwich with lettuce surrounded by potato chips and a pickle. Sure looked better than the thin peanut butter sandwiches I'd been fixing for myself.

"How's your dad doing?"

I shrugged. "Fine."

"I heard Mark Zimmerman is coming home in July. Maybe he'll make it for the July Fourth festival."

I'd heard about that festival in church. "Who's Mark Zimmerman?"

"Oh, I thought maybe you knew the family. Mark's in Vietnam."

"Nope." I chowed down.

"Maybe your dad has met his parents. They go to your church."

Yeah, now I remembered. *The local boy.* Mark Zimmerman. I nodded thoughtfully. I felt relieved knowing that someone everyone liked was coming home. That would show them that recruiters weren't bad people.

"So what's been going on with you?" she asked between bites. "What have you been up to?"

"You know, just hanging around." Salt and vinegar potato chips—my favorite.

"What about those boys you met? Have you been playing with them?"

I thought of Ray, but then stupid Prater took over. "I only saw them that one day," I said. "I'm kind of busy anyway. You know, with Jack and all."

"Hmm." Millie nodded slowly. She sipped her coffee, set it down, and grabbed her purse. Then she pulled out some money and handed it to me. "After lunch, I want you to go on over to Tysko's. You know where that is?"

I nodded; it was the corner grocery store just past Ray's house.

"I want you to get an ice cream cone. There's enough there for two."

"You want me to bring you back one?" That would be hard; it would melt and run down my hand.

Millie laughed. "Not me, honey, I'm trying to lose weight! You go and treat your friend to ice cream." She sat back in her chair.

Great idea! Who could say no to ice cream? I stuffed the money into my pocket. "Thanks, Millie," I said, smiling. She smiled, too, already back to her sandwich; I gobbled down the rest of mine. Maybe after ice cream, Ray and I could play basketball or something.

I screeched my chair back and slid my dishes on the counter. "Is it okay, can I go now?"

Millie held up one finger and swallowed. Then she said, "The turtle sundae is excellent."

I got on my bike and kept Jack on my right side. That way, I could keep him safe from cars. He trotted along; running was just about his favorite thing. There was no breeze today and no clouds, just the sun beating down on us. Heat rose from the tar. That ice cream was sure going to be good.

As we coasted around the bend, I saw Ray yo-yoing in his driveway.

"Ray!" I shouted.

An old lady with puffy hair sat on the porch of the house before Ray's. She startled when I yelled. I caught a glimpse of black and white jumping off her lap—a cat, I think. "Sorry!" I called out but kept going. I pedaled faster and skidded to a stop in Ray's driveway.

"Hiya!" he said. He patted Jack's head, then stood, threw the yo-yo down, and whipped it around the opposite finger. The yo-yo landed on the string still spinning. "Man on trapeze."

"Cool," I said. "Can you do walk-the-dog?"

Ray laughed. "Beginner's trick." But he did it anyway. Jack sniffed an imaginary trail left by the yo-yo before Ray pulled it up.

"I can never do that with my yo-yo—it just comes right back up."

He cupped his yo-yo and nodded. "You probably have one of those yo-yos that's tied around the axle. Mine's got a slip string—"

Just then the screen door banged and Prater barged out holding a basketball. Oh, man. Why does he have to be here?

"Hey, kid!" Prater called, clobbering down the stairs. "Shoot any squirrels lately?"

Real funny. "About as many as you have."

He smirked but pulled up fast when he saw Jack.

"What's wrong?" I asked. I couldn't help myself—I wanted to mess with him after the way he acted the other day. I laid my bike down and walked closer to Prater with Jack.

He shuffled backward. He didn't take his eyes off Jack. His hand fumbled behind him, raking the air for the porch rail.

All of a sudden, shame washed over me. I knew Prater's weak spot, and I was using Jack as a weapon to hit it. That was wrong on both parts. Prater had been a jerk with the guns, but I remembered how he'd let me pet his horse—how he didn't make fun of me when I thought the horse was going to bite me.

I didn't *really* want him to be afraid of Jack. I wanted him to *like* Jack. Besides, Jack was a good dog. I stooped, pretending to fix his collar. Without looking at Prater I said, "Come on over here and pet him. He won't bite."

Prater spoke in a quiet voice. "I thought we were going to play twenty-one."

"Yeah, in a second," Ray said, coming up to Jack. Jack greeted him by snuffling into his hand. "Jack won't hurt you."

"I know that!" Prater snapped. He huffed and puffed for a second. "Geez! What's the big deal?" Shaking his head, he took a few wary steps closer.

Jack growled.

Prater jumped back. "I knew it! He's an attack dog!"

"No, he's not!" I tried to calm my voice. "Look," I said, "bend down so you're not looming over him. When you stick out your hand, make a loose fist and hold it out so he can sniff it."

Prater licked his lips and swallowed before following my instructions. I let the leash out a little and Jack moved toward him, giving his tail a faint wag. When Jack's nose touched his hand, Prater stiffened and squeezed his eyes shut.

Jack's muscles tensed and he barked.

Prater scrambled backward. "What's wrong with him?"

"Dogs can sense fear," I started. "He probably—"

"I'm not afraid!" He stood and made a wide arc around us to the driveway. "I just don't like him, okay? Stupid dog."

I pulled Jack closer to me. "He's not stupid."

"Alan, just be more relaxed, like with Shadow," Ray said.

Prater stood and shoved his hands into his pockets. "Who cares? I don't care; he's just a weird dog, that's all."

I pressed my lips together. I wished I had never come here.

"Jack's not weird," Ray said and laughed. "You are." He chucked Prater on the shoulder.

"Yeah, right," Prater said, returning a light punch.

Ray looked at me. "You want to shoot baskets, then? We could play twenty-one or horse."

I jammed my hand into my pocket, fingering the bills. There was probably enough for three cones. Not that I wanted Prater along, but I couldn't invite Ray without asking Prater, too. Maybe this would work out. If I bought him ice cream, he might be nicer to me. Maybe he would like me better. Maybe he would like Jack better.

"Millie gave me money for ice cream," I said. "She said I could treat you." I looked at Prater. "Both of you."

chapter 11

Tysko's sat on the corner down from Ray's house. We rode past a farmer driving a tractor on the road and turned into the parking lot. Picnic tables sat in front of the store and it looked like a lot of people had the same idea as we did. We leaned our bikes against a table and hurried into line just as a lady was getting her cone.

When she stepped away from the window, I had eyes only on her triple scoop with sprinkles; I didn't notice Jack snuffling up to her legs.

She let out a jagged sound of surprise and backed up so quickly, one vanilla scoop plopped onto the ground. No hesitation on Jack's part—he immediately started lapping it up.

I looked at her face. She wasn't that old, maybe in her twenties. "Sorry about that," I said. "He was just trying to be friendly."

"He scared the heck out of me," she said. She smiled, but her body tensed against the serving window.

An older woman leaned out and spoke to me like a teacher. "Better hold your dog a little closer, okay?"

"Yes, ma'am." I was just about to offer to pay for that scoop when the older woman said she'd give the girl a whole new cone.

When she got it, she edged away in the direction opposite of Jack. It bothered me. I wanted to fix her impression of him. "He won't bite," I said.

She laughed at herself and shrugged, walking away.

"Guess she's scared of dogs," Prater said.

Oh, yeah. He left that wide open. A million zingers sprang to mind, but I didn't let any of them loose. I wanted this afternoon to work out. Whatever Prater's problem was, I was hoping the ice cream would help solve it. So even if he didn't know it, not saying anything was the second nice thing I did for him. Buying the ice cream was the first.

Three double scoops sent us to the picnic table we'd parked our bikes next to. Prater sat opposite me, at another table facing us. He was as far away from Jack as he could get while still sitting by Ray. I looped Jack's leash around my handlebars a couple of times and set down a cup of water for him.

We didn't talk for a few minutes, too busy eating our ice cream. Jack lapped some of the water, and then sat straight, watching and listening. Some little kids ran laughing around another table. Their mom had a baby on her lap, and ice cream smeared his face like a chocolate beard.

"So you're going to that show, then?" Ray asked Prater. He had to turn away from me to do this, Prater had separated himself so well.

"Yeah, Blackbeard's in it."

"Is Blackbeard one of your horses?" I asked.

Prater twisted his cone for a better angle. "One of our *champion* horses."

"That's cool." I bit into a chunk of butter pecan and my front teeth froze. "Do you ride them in the shows?"

"I ride Alexander; he's a quarter horse, but my dad rides Blackbeard, and my uncle rides The Great White North."

"What?" A grin crossed my face.

"That's the horse's show name," Ray said. "The Great White North."

"But we call him Pete."

"Pete? The Great White North is *Pete*?" It seemed funny to call a horse Pete. The show name sounded so much more powerful.

Prater was down to his last scoop. "Guess what color he is?"

It seemed obvious, but maybe it was a joke, like how that bald guy on *The Three Stooges* was named Curly. I went for it anyway. "White?"

Prater nodded, swallowed his ice cream.

"You should see all the trophies they have," Ray said to me.

"Yep," Prater said, warming to the subject. "And Shadow is next." I realized he was talking to me like maybe I was a friend. Yep, the ice cream was definitely a move in the right direction.

Ray nodded. "I bet—"

All of a sudden, Jack whined and strained against the leash. Snapping and growling, he reared up on his hind legs, then he jumped and bolted. The bikes fell like dominoes and the leash slipped out. Jack tore across the parking lot like a torpedo.

I shot out of my seat. "Jack!"

He ran through the grass on the other side and I saw a small dark shape scuttle through the weeds. Then, with me and everyone else watching, Jack leaped through the grass and clamped his jaws down on a rabbit. Some ladies gasped and one covered her eyes with both hands. "Look at what that dog did!" a little boy shouted. A tiny girl at the next table started crying.

Jack trotted toward me with the body in his jaws, the rabbit's lifeless head flopping with each step. "Oh, oh," a woman moaned. Some of the ladies pulled their kids back in tight arms as Jack passed between the tables. Jack's ears were erect and flushed with a deep rose color. I stood, frozen. Ray and Prater were also standing.

Jack stopped in front of me, laid the rabbit down, and looked up expectantly.

"Whoa!" Prater said. "A kill." When he peered over to inspect, Jack lowered his head and snarled. Prater snapped upright. "Geez!"

"That dog killed a bunny rabbit!" a boy shrieked.

"Come over here, Troy!" the lady with the baby shouted.

Loud wails and sobs came from the little girl. Her mother held her tightly while staring right at me. "What's wrong with you?" she shouted across the tables. "You don't bring a dog like that around children."

"Joshua," murmured Ray. I couldn't respond. "Come on, Josh, we have to do something."

"Let's get out of here," Prater said. He'd finished his cone and was now mounting his bike.

Jack remained at my feet, his offering before him.

Some of the little kids had gathered on the other side of the picnic area and shouted their version of what happened. "He growled like a lion." "He's got rabies!" "He tried to eat me but I ran too fast."

I crouched and held Jack's leash. Blood pooled under the rabbit's neck. I felt sick and hollow. I looked into Jack's face, but I saw no meanness—he was still Jack.

One of the ladies marched over to us, her eyes narrow as slits and her hands clenched. "Get that vicious dog out of here before I call the police," she said. "What are your names?" She sounded like a teacher.

"It's *his* dog," Prater said and pointed at me. He put one foot on the pedal, ready to make his escape. "He's your crazy dog—no wonder he was at the pound." I looked at him, speechless.

"Shut up," Ray said.

I was still crouching beside Jack. Would she really call the police? Could they take Jack away?

Ray glanced at his house and then at me. "We could bury the rabbit in my yard. I'll go get a shovel."

I stood up and nodded. Ray crossed the side street to his house. Prater pressed down on his pedals, standing as he rode. "Later, gator," he called out.

The angry lady stepped forward. She looked down and her lips pulled back in disgust. "Keep that dog in a pen, or I *will* call the police next time." She spun around and joined the other mothers ushering their kids into their cars.

I was alone. I tied Jack up to a nearby table, pulling the knots hard and checking them. Bending down, I touched the rabbit's back. It was soft and still warm. It should have been out playing, not lying dead here on the concrete. My first time touching a rabbit. I wished I could be petting him alive.

Ray came back with a shovel and a piece of cardboard. I held the cardboard down while Ray used the shovel to push the rabbit over. Its body rumpled, like an old doll that had lost some of its stuffing. The ice cream I'd just eaten turned sour in my stomach. Ray laid down the shovel and picked up the cardboard, and I untied Jack, wrapped the leash around my fist, and grabbed the shovel with the other hand. We walked in silence the short distance to his house.

"Let's go around up here," Ray said, motioning with his chin to the far corner of his house, the side that shared a space with that old lady's house. "Easier to get to the shed."

As we passed, the old lady watched us with disapproving eyes. "Hi, Mrs. Brenner," Ray said. She tilted forward on the rocker, taking in the scene while clutching the black-and-white cat in her arms.

She shook her knobby finger at me. My heart beat double time and I quickly looked away from her, but that didn't stop what she said next. "He's a devil dog. Yella eyes, ears like horns—I saw what he did." She leaned back, puckered her face, and spoke from her chair like a judge giving a sentence. *"Devil dog."*

I swallowed and bent my head. "Did you hear what she said?" I whispered to Ray as we walked into the shady area behind his shed.

"Don't worry about her," Ray said. "She sits all day with that cat, just watching what everyone does. No one pays any attention to her."

I tried not to pay attention either, but I couldn't help it.

Ray got another shovel while I cinched Jack's leash around a tree. As we dug, thoughts tumbled around in my head— Jack, a devil dog; bloody rabbit fur; all those people yelling at me. *I'll call the police.*

My eyes watered. I kept my face down as I worked. It felt

weird to throw dirt on top of the rabbit. I remembered hearing about how, in the old days, they buried people with a string in their coffin. The string led up to a bell above the ground. If the dead person wasn't really dead, they could ring the bell and someone would dig them out. But I knew the rabbit was dead. I had pressed my hand on him and felt no heartbeat, no breathing.

Ray patted the last chunk of grass over the little grave. Wiping his forehead with his arm, he said, "Well, that's it, then."

I sighed. "Yeah."

He put the shovels in the shed, I untied Jack, and we plopped down on the steps of the back porch.

My head hung down. "I can't believe he did that."

"Yeah," Ray said. "But he didn't really do anything wrong."

"What do you mean? He killed that rabbit."

Ray scratched Jack's ears. "We used to have a cat that would leave dead birds at the front door," Ray said. "My mom said that was the cat's way of taking care of us, like he was trying to feed us."

"Really?"

"Yeah, so that's like what Jack was doing."

I leaned back and thought about that for a minute. The whole scene replayed in my head: Jack, still tied to the bike, trying to tell me he saw something. Instead of paying attention to him, I was busy listening to Prater, trying to get in good with him. Well, that didn't really work. One word from those ladies and Prater had no problem pointing his finger at me. On top of that, he didn't even say thank you for the ice cream. Then he took off, saving his own skin.

But not Ray, who sat beside me now, stretched out along the steps with Jack pushed into his side. I didn't know if he was a fast runner like Scott, but I knew I could be friends with him. Even if it meant dealing with Prater.

chapter 12

Dad was not happy when I told him what happened. He stared at Jack lying in the middle of the living room floor and shook his head. "Did he go near any of the kids? Did he threaten them?"

"No! All he did was chase a rabbit and bring it to me." I didn't tell Dad how shocked I'd felt. "Just like how cats leave birds for their owners."

He turned and leveled his eyes at me. "Jack is a lot different from a cat. Look at him—he's wiry, he's got those ears, that pointy face—"

"So what?"

Dad raised his eyebrows. "So what? We're lucky he didn't attack a kid."

"He would never do that!" Jack yawned, his jaws opening

wide. He let out a squeaky sound. I gestured toward him. "You *know* he would never do that."

Sighing, Dad leaned back on the couch. "I don't think he would either. But I can see how other people might think that." He crossed his arms. "Maybe we *should* build him a pen."

"No way!" I said. "I don't want him stuck in a cage all the time." The sound of the news program on TV filtered in, and I heard the reporter say they were rolling the antiwar protest from earlier in the day.

"We have to do *something.*" Dad's attention wavered between me and the television. "We can't live with this commotion all the time." He focused on me. "First the trash cans, now this—we're not making good neighbors, I can tell you that right now."

"You want to put him in jail because of the neighbors?"

Dad rolled his eyes. "Don't be so dramatic. I'm not saying put him in jail. He just needs to be . . ." He paused, searching for a word. "Contained."

"But *not* in a cage."

He leaned against the arm of the couch and rubbed his chin with his fingers. "I can put up a run for him in the backyard—I'll give him enough line to cover the yard without leaving it. What do you think?"

I could live with that.

My gaze drifted to the TV. A bunch of guys and girls waved hand-painted signs: MAKE LOVE, NOT WAR. EIGHTEEN TODAY, DEAD TOMORROW. A couple of guys came up behind the reporter and shouted, "One, two, three, four; we don't want your *bleeping* war!" Even with the bleep, it wasn't hard to figure out what they'd said.

The picture flashed back to the newsroom, and they played a newsreel from the war. Our soldiers advanced through tangled-looking woods and palm trees. No choppers in the air, only blue sky. If you just looked up, you wouldn't even know there was a war.

Then the scene cut to soldiers rushing out from a ditch. One soldier ran right past the camera. His face was dirty and had cuts on it.

"More than forty-five thousand American soldiers have lost their lives so far in Vietnam," the anchorman said. Two soldiers crossed the television screen carrying a dead soldier on a stretcher. Blood splattered over his eyes; his ear was obliterated. "Loved ones at home want to know if the sacrifice is worth it."

Dad pressed his fingers to his eyes. I turned the TV off.

"Dad?" I lay on the floor beside Jack.

From behind his hand, Dad answered. "Yeah?"

"Is that guy—what happened to that MIA guy?"

He lowered his head. "I called the family the other day, talked with the father. They don't know anything. I told him I'd try to help." He put his hand down and looked at me. "The father's retired army. His older son did a tour in 'Nam a couple of years ago."

I'd absentmindedly stopped petting Jack as I listened, so

he rolled over and pawed to get me started again. One father and two sons in the army. Some families were like that—it just ran in their blood. Dad never talked about me going in and I didn't know if I wanted to. I mean, I thought about it sometimes, especially when we went to air shows and the Thunderbirds roared in formation over our heads, blasting out our eardrums with the power of their engines. But when I saw things like that dead soldier—or even the other soldiers running to the fight with their guns—it scared me to think about really being there.

Fumbling behind me, I grabbed Jack's toy and threw it. He leaped up, his legs tangled for a second like a baby deer's, then he ran after the toy and brought it back. Dropping it, he backed up a step and took on a ready position. I faked him out to the left, then threw it right.

The government said we were over there to protect democracy. That sounded like a good thing. I didn't understand why people were against that. I didn't understand why, just a couple of months ago, the news showed all these veterans from the war tearing off their medals and throwing them on the ground in Washington DC. They earned those medals by being brave. One soldier said he was ashamed of what his country made him do. It was all mixed up.

More parents had been calling Dad the past couple weeks to yell at him for talking to their sons about the air force. "I know you don't want to hear this," I heard him say to one parent, "but there's a war going on. He's got no deferment. I believe the air force will give him the best of all options."

Dad always looked drained after these phone calls, like he did a few minutes ago watching the news. I determined right then that Jack wouldn't be turned into a problem. I would keep him in line. I would stick up for him. If I could, I'd stick up for Dad, too. I'd slam the phone down on those people yelling at him. *He has medals, too*, I'd yell. *He was in the Korean War.*

No one wants to fight, but sometimes you have no choice.

chapter 13

Dad and I were in the driveway, washing and waxing our new Gran Torino. Well, not exactly ours—the air force had given it to Dad because of all the driving he had to do as a recruiter. Definitely cooler than the old station wagon. The Torino's steel-blue coat gleamed in the sun and the hubcaps shone like mirrors. And if that weren't cool enough, the air force insignia on the driver's side made the car look way important.

Jack kept us company on the run Dad had put up for him. Tiny bubbles floated out of the bottle of dish soap when I squeezed it. Jack tried to eat them.

The mailman saw us by the car and walked up the driveway. He handed the mail to Dad and talked for a minute before walking away.

"Bills, bills, bills," Dad said as he riffled through the envelopes. "Hmm, here's something for you." He handed me a letter. "ADBA, wonder what that is."

"ADBA?" My heart leaped. "The dog club!" I snatched the letter out of his hand and tore it open.

Dear Joshua,

I was very excited when I received your letter and the picture of your dog, Jack. Jack is a Pharaoh hound, a rare breed in the United States. The president of the Royal Hounds Club of America told me that a Mrs. Weiss, who lived in your area, imported a Pharaoh hound about a year ago. Unfortunately, Mrs. Weiss recently passed away. There was no record of the dog's sale after her death. After comparing Jack's photo to a photo of Mrs. Weiss's hound, I am certain they are the same dog.

You have a very special dog there! Pharaohs are extremely loyal and affectionate. They are fierce hunters, hunting by scent as well as sight. Jack's ancestry goes all the way back to the hounds in King Tut's palace. These dogs were valued for their ability to put meat on the table. The glowing ears you mentioned are a characteristic distinctive to Pharaoh hounds.

I'm glad Jack found a home with someone who

loves him. Here's something you might find interesting: Jack's first name was Sweet Prince William.

> *Sincerely,*
> *Eugene Morrows*
> *Regional President, American Dog Breeders*
> *Association*

I read the letter again and again.

"What is it?" Dad asked.

"I . . . it's a . . ." I handed the letter to him.

He scanned it quickly, then smiled and handed it back to me. "Well, I'll be," he said. "That's really something."

I looked at Jack in amazement. *Sweet Prince William.* This news was too big, too excellent. "Can I go to Ray's house?" I blurted.

"He's out back with Alan," Ray's mom said, holding the screen door open. I choked back a groan. Why did *he* have to be here? But maybe that was a good thing. He'd hear that Jack was a purebred, and that Jack's ancestors could be traced all the way to the palace of King Tut. Bet he couldn't say that about any of his *horses.*

Mrs. Miller held out a plate of peanut butter cookies, the kind you press a fork on to make hash marks. I took two. She must have just baked them because they were warm, and the peanut-butter smell left a trail in the air. "Just go around the side of the house, okay?" She smiled and bit into a cookie.

I broke off a tiny chunk for Jack before biting into one myself. Oh, man, so good. And it didn't have nuts in it; I hate them in cookies or brownies.

Speaking of nuts, Prater was sitting on the concrete pad at the back of Ray's house. I bit into the second cookie and looked around, but I didn't see Ray.

I tried to act casual. "Where's Ray?" I asked, causing Prater to startle. I smirked before realizing it.

He clucked his tongue. "How come every time I see you, you're eating?" he said. He held something that looked like a nail, and he had a piece of leather on a cardboard in front of him.

Okay, so this was how it was going to be. I made my voice flat. "Do you know where Ray is?"

"Yeah," he said, picking up a mallet. "We're doing something."

Well, duh. Everyone's *doing* something, even if it's just breathing. Jack and I stepped closer. Prater was making some kind of drawing on the leather.

He shrank away from us, his eyes flitting over Jack. "Don't come over here! You almost made me make a mistake."

We weren't even that close. But I backed away from him anyway, tied the leash to the railing, and sat on the stoop with Jack to wait for Ray. Jack panted while looking at me expectantly. *What's next?* his eyes said. *What're we doing?* I ruffled his ears to let him know it was okay—we were just waiting for a few minutes.

On the concrete, Prater seemed to have forgotten us. He dragged something that looked like a screwdriver across the leather, and thin strips rippled up. Brushing them aside, he repeated what he did, then picked up a different tool and turned it on the leather in short strokes. The tip of his tongue stuck out between his lips.

The back door creaked open. "Hey," Ray said as he ambled down the steps. "What's going on?"

I pulled the letter from the dog club out of my back pocket. I couldn't help smiling as I handed him the envelope. "Look what I got!"

He slipped the letter out and began to read. "Wow," he said, glancing up for a second. I liked that he sounded impressed.

"What is it?" Prater demanded.

I shrugged. "Something about Jack." Something *great* about Jack.

He laid his stuff down and stood beside Ray. I could see his lips moving as he read over Ray's shoulder.

"Give me that." Prater snatched the letter from Ray.

"Don't tear it," I said and tried to grab it.

Prater jerked his hand away and finished reading the letter. Then he started laughing, a fake, overly hearty laugh. "You got some dead old lady's dog!"

How did he do that? How was he able to make everything sound so stupid?

Ray said, "That's not what it says."

"Yes, it does." His eyes gleamed—this was fun to him.

I clenched my teeth. "Give it back to me," I said and held out my hand for the letter.

He snapped his arm back, holding the letter out of my reach. A challenging smile spread across his face.

I lunged, nearly falling, and Jack let out an uncertain woof. He pulled against the leash, stretching it to its full length.

Prater focused on Jack. "He better not get loose."

"So what if he did?" I countered, though I didn't want Jack to get loose either.

"Oh, my God," Ray said, treading toward Prater. "Give me the letter; you grabbed it before I had a chance to finish it."

Ray made a move for it, but Prater dodged him, laughing.

I took a step closer to Prater. "You're just jealous."

"I'm not jealous!" He snorted. "I don't even care about your stupid dog."

"Then give me the letter."

His eyes lit up. "Then come and get it."

I sprinted across the grass, and as I did, I stumbled over his tools, heard something crack, and knocked over the bowl of water.

Prater's mouth fell open. "You did that on purpose!"

"I did not!" I said, and at the same time, Ray said, "No, he didn't."

Prater looked from me to Ray and back to me again. He picked up the now-soaked leather, scowling. "*I* was just playing around, but *you* did it on purpose. You ruined it," he said, shaking the water from the leather. "This was going to be a present for my aunt." Then he scanned the grass. "You broke my best knife!"

"It was an accident," Ray said. "You should've given him the letter."

Prater's eyes constricted, and before I could stop him, he tore the letter into long shreds and threw them down. "There you go," he spat. "There's your precious letter."

My mouth fell open, then clinched shut. I stared disbelievingly at the pieces by his feet.

"Oh, man," Ray said. "You didn't have to do that."

Prater lifted one shoulder. He answered Ray but stared at me. "Now we're even." The set of his jaw challenged me to do something.

Every neuron in my brain fired like pistons—hit him, hit him! And I wanted to. My hands curled into fists and my blood boiled. But then the scene flashed by me like a movie: I shove him; he hits me; I punch him back. A bloody nose or a black eye later, his knife is still broken, and my letter is still ripped. Fighting wouldn't change that. Fighting wouldn't settle whatever was between Prater and me.

I took a step toward him and he braced himself. Then I leaned down and picked up the pieces by his feet.

As much as I wanted to, I didn't leave. Leaving would feel like running away, as if I were backing down to Prater, and there was no way I was going to do that. As I scooped up the last shred of paper, I relaxed the muscles in my face and turned to Ray with an almost pleasant expression. "Hey," I said, keeping my voice light, "do you have any tape?"

chapter 14

The letter lay on Ray's kitchen table. Lucky for me—if you can call it that—Prater had ripped the letter into strips. I'd been able to tape them back together like a puzzle.

"What's his problem?" I asked when Mrs. Miller left the kitchen. I ironed the letter flat with my hand. Mrs. Miller had this huge cutting board and rows of cookies lay cooling on it. The whole kitchen filled with the warm scent of peanut butter and sugar.

Ray stood and glanced through the window. Prater was still out there, starting on a new piece of leather. I'd worried about leaving Jack anywhere near him, but Ray insisted Prater wouldn't do anything to Jack.

Ray sat, opened his mouth to say something, then shook his head and looked down.

"What?"

"Well . . ." He closed his mouth again.

He wanted to tell me and he didn't want to tell me, but I definitely wanted to know.

"Come on, I won't say anything."

When someone's about to spill, all their fidgeting stops. They kind of lean toward you, and they level their eyes with yours, making a bridge of trust. That's what Ray did now.

"Remember when CeeCee said Alan is scared of dogs?"

"Yeah . . ." I fiddled with the bottle cap from the pop Ray gave me, spinning it across the table and catching it. Never look eager when you're waiting to hear a secret; it makes the other person anxious, like maybe they should just keep quiet.

He stared straight at me. "You can't tell him I told you this."

Mrs. Miller rounded the corner. Man, she walked quietly. Ray shook his head. *Be quiet.*

Mrs. Miller had fixed a bandanna around her hair and was carrying a dusting rag, which she set on the counter. She was probably around the same age my mom would've been. I wondered if they might have become friends.

"What're you boys doing in already?" she asked as she loaded the percolator with water and coffee. She didn't seem to need an answer. Looking through the window above the sink, she chuckled. "Alan's such a perfectionist."

Well, I could think of a few other words to describe him.

She lit the stove and flames encircled the coffeepot. Leaning against the counter, she brushed back some loose hair with her hand. "So how are you and your dad doing?"

Oh, no. Any other time, talk to me any other time, but not when I'm about to hear Prater's biggest secret. "Fine," I said. Adults like to hear positive things. But they also like details. "My dad just got a new car from the air force."

"Ooh!" she said approvingly. "Good for him!" She whisked up her rag and padded out of the kitchen.

I pressed the edge of the bottle cap into my palm and looked at the zigzag impression it made. "So you were saying?" I prompted Ray. "Something about Alan being scared of dogs?"

"You *can't* tell him I told you." He emphasized his words by widening his eyes. I shook my head quickly. Heaving a big sigh, he said, "When he was six, one of his dad's friends brought his big dogs with him to go hunting. Alan was outside, alone with the dogs, when one of them attacked him."

He clasped his pop bottle. "I was supposed to be there. He wanted me to go, but I didn't want to. Anyway, the dog bit his head, tore part of an earlobe, and ripped his side open. My uncle had to beat the dog off; it wouldn't stop. Alan was in the hospital for a few days."

Mrs. Miller called out from the other room. "Ray, get me the Pledge, okay?"

"Okay," he called back.

After he left the room, I couldn't stop thinking about

Prater. The whole time Ray had been talking, it happened in front of my eyes like a movie. I imagined him about the size of CeeCee, terrified and bloodied by a ferocious dog, no one around to help. No wonder he was scared of Jack.

When Ray came back and sat down, I asked, "What happened to the dog?"

"Uncle Bruce and his friend shot him."

I nodded. You couldn't keep a dog like that—it might've killed Prater if his dad hadn't come out in time. I folded the letter, rubbing my finger along the creases to settle the tape. We sat there, as what Ray had just said played in our thoughts. The coffeepot percolated, making clanky metal sounds and filling the room with the dark smell of coffee.

Ray cracked his knuckles, one by one. "Don't tell him I told you."

I frowned and shook my head. "So you think that's why he ripped up my letter?"

"No, he ripped it up because you stepped on his knife and you also got that leather really wet."

"But it was an accident!"

"Yeah, but he doesn't think so."

Mrs. Miller strolled in and tousled Ray's hair. "Someone needs a haircut!" Ray smirked and shook off her hand. A pang of sadness hit me. I deflected it by thinking of something else, anything else.

"Hey," I said to Ray, "can you show me some of those yo-yo tricks?"

"Yeah!" He leaped up from his chair, but then his mom caught his arm.

"Don't forget about Alan," she said, then turned to pour herself a cup of coffee.

Ray rolled his eyes. "I'm just going to get my yo-yos and we'll go outside."

"Good." She sipped her coffee.

Actually, it *was* good we were going back outside. I didn't want to lose face with Prater, and even more important, I didn't want to leave Jack alone with him too long. Mrs. Miller went back to her chores, and when Ray came in with his yo-yos, I said, "He'll probably be mad at you for coming inside with me." It was a fact that he was already mad at *me*.

Ray pocketed one yo-yo, looped the other, and threw it down. "He couldn't stay mad too long. He doesn't really have any other friends."

I sat up straighter and leaned forward. "What do you mean?"

"Well, you know, he's always, like, picking on people."

"He doesn't pick on you."

"He always makes fun of me because of the yo-yo. My mom says he's jealous, but she's wrong. He thinks it's stupid. I'm sick of it."

"My mom always said to ignore people like that."

"My mom says that, too." He wove the string around his fingers and looped it around his thumb. "Shooting star," he said.

I could see it. "Cool!"

Ray gave a little grin and shrugged. He dropped the star and brought the yo-yo up into his hand. "I never make fun of the stuff he does. Some cousin."

I had seen the way Prater treated Ray. To him, they were more than just cousins—they were best friends. Which would be okay, except he didn't want Ray to be friends with anyone else. "I thought you guys were best friends."

"No." He shook his head. "Just cousins. Our mothers are always putting us together because *they* are best friends." He seemed to think about that for a second. "I mean, we *are* friends. I just—well, sometimes he can be a real butthead, you know?"

Exactly. Except the word that came to my mind was shorter and more precise.

chapter 15

We decided to build a fort.

The idea came up during Sunday school in notes Ray and I passed back and forth. I knew exactly where we should do it. *By the arrowheads*, I scribbled just before class got out. *Come to my house after lunch.* Prater never attended Sunday school and only half the time did his family come to church, something I was glad for because then I could make plans with Ray without Prater butting in.

Now Ray and I stood in the woods deciding how to construct the fort. Jack lay on the ground close by, his leash looped tightly around a tree.

"We could put up a hut like on *Gilligan's Island*," I said.

"Or a tree house." Ray pointed to a cluster of trees.

I bent down to a blueberry bush and popped one in my mouth. Mmm, sweet now. "Hey, what if we dig part of it?"

I remembered seeing soldiers hiding in foxholes on television. "Then we could cover the top and make a secret entrance."

"Yeah," Ray said. "Like camouflage."

I ran back to the house for shovels while Ray cleared the sticks and stuff out of the way. When we first thrust the shovels into the ground, it was like trying to dig concrete. It wasn't long before we decided to take a break. Jack pranced in circles as I untied his leash and wound it around my hand. "Let's go!" I patted his side.

Jack yipped and we took off. The trees blurred as we raced by them. We pounded up the mountain and sailed over a tree stump, and I ducked when we passed under a low branch. Jack and I took the mountain like soldiers racing through an obstacle course. Then Jack caught scent of something and made a line drive through the woods.

"Wait!" Ray called.

"Jack, stop." I tried to slow him down but he pulled me forward, intent on his prey. I glanced downhill to Ray. He was bending over slightly, bracing his hands on his knees; his chest was heaving.

"Stop, Jack," I said and tugged at the leash. He stopped but huffed and strained against the leash to continue his charge. I pulled him in closer. "C'mon, boy, we have to wait for Ray." He groaned in frustration, but I held firm and he gave up the chase. We trotted down to Ray, who was still trying to catch his breath.

"Man!" he said between gasps. "How fast can you run?"

I shrugged my shoulders. "I don't know," I said and grinned. "As fast as Jack makes me."

"You're, like, in the Olympics or something."

I laughed.

"Okay," Ray said, straightening up. "I'm ready."

Jack pulled me as we zigzagged across the mountain. He veered at an angle we'd never followed before. I was holding back a little, making Jack go slower. I didn't want Ray to feel bad, and plus it was more fun if we could all do it together. We ran without talking; only our footsteps sounded through the woods.

Suddenly, Jack stopped. I sensed where we were on the mountain, but we had never been on this side before. Whatever Jack had been tracing was lost to him; he now pranced after a yellow butterfly that flitted by.

"Hey," Ray said, walking ahead of us. The trees thinned in that direction, like there was a clearing on the other side. Ray stopped before the edge of the trees and hunkered down. "C'mere," he whispered.

"Come on, Jack," I said quietly. We crept up to Ray and crouched beside him.

"Alan's backyard," Ray whispered.

I nodded. From our hiding place, we could see down through the woods to Prater's tree house. It was finished now. Trim decorated the doorways and windows, and the whole thing was perfectly square. His tree house looked exactly like a dollhouse. I shifted back on my feet. It was weird, spying on him like this, even though I didn't see him anywhere. Still, I didn't like being here—I didn't want to get caught.

"Let's go," I said.

Dad was tinkering in the garage when we got back. Before Ray left, we went up to my room and I pulled out my Pennsylvania shoe box. I had planned this moment from the time we decided to build a fort, and especially since we didn't find any more arrowheads in our digging.

I laid the arrowheads on the carpet in front of me. The points were a bit rounded off, but that could have been from all that time in the ground. One of them was a little bigger than the other. I picked it up and rubbed it with my thumb. "The last person to touch this was an Indian," I said to Ray. "You can have it."

Ray reached for it. He turned the arrowhead over in his hand a few times and looked up. "Wow." His voice was solemn, respectful. I wondered if he imagined the brave as I did. "I can keep it?" he asked.

"Yep." It was, for both of us, a serious gesture. Giving away a thing of such importance meant something. He'd stuck up for me more than once, so he rightly deserved an arrowhead.

"Thanks, man. I'll take good care of it."

I reached under my bed and pulled out a wooden recorder. "Let us now smoke the peace pipe."

I tooted on the recorder. Jack's ears perked. I gave the recorder another good toot and Jack howled like he was trying to harmonize. Ray and I laughed. He slipped his hand over Jack's head and then took his turn on the recorder, accompanied by Jack. Jack's lips formed a perfect O.

"Look," I said. "Look at Jack!" But even our laughing did not interrupt Jack's soulful baying. His mournful sound seemed ancient and primitive to me, like it was part of this mountain and these arrowheads and a history of things that only Jack knew. I put the recorder down and stroked Jack gently until he stopped.

chapter 16

" 'The Trouble with Tribbles,' " Millie answered. We sat at the table, lingering over our apple pie and debating the best *Star Trek* episode. Jack lay under the table, hoping for crumbs.

"No way! It's 'A Piece of the Action!' " Best episode ever.

Millie pressed her fork into the pie crumbs on her plate. "Which one is that?"

"The one where Kirk and Spock pretend to be gangsters in order to get the people on this other planet to stop fighting each other."

"Oh, yeah." She nodded. "But I like the Tribbles one better. It's cute."

Well, that's what we want in our science fiction—cute. The gangster one was better. Still, I couldn't believe Millie was such a big fan of *Star Trek*. I was about to ask her what else she liked about the show when Dad pushed open the back door and slung his briefcase on the counter.

"Hey, Dad—which Star Trek—"

Jack nearly turned over the table when he jumped out to greet Dad. I had to hold down my milk glass. Jack danced around Dad, yipping and pawing him, sniffing his feet.

But Dad didn't lean to pet him like he usually did. His face was slack, his eyes rimmed in red. His whole body slumped with exhaustion. Sitting down, he dropped his head into his hands, raking his hair with his fingers.

My heart struck a fast beat. I'd seen him like this only once before and that's when the doctor told us about Mom's cancer. My voice cracked when I asked, "Dad—what's wrong?"

Millie rose and patted his back.

"I talked with Stan Kowalski today. He got a visit from an NCO and the army chaplain—"

"No!" Millie clutched her arms to her chest.

Dad lifted his head and stared into space. "David was killed in action. They'll be flying his body back."

"Oh, dear Lord." Millie's hands flapped in the air. "Poor Jan. Oh, my gosh . . ." Tears rolled down her face. She pulled a tissue from her apron pocket and wiped her cheeks.

The muscles in Dad's jaw flexed. His eyebrows pressed down and he squeezed his eyes shut. "I drove over to their house." He looked up at Millie. It seemed as though he were pleading or searching. "They lost their son . . ."

Bewilderment filled his eyes. I was younger when Mom died; I knew only how sad I was. Now seeing the grief on Dad's face, I didn't know what to do. Someone died. He wasn't related to us, but he was connected somehow. He was connected through death.

Millie reached out and hugged Dad, and he let her.

Jack laid his head over my feet. I couldn't believe that guy—*David*—I couldn't believe *David* had died. I didn't have to wonder what his family was doing right now; I knew firsthand. *This can't be real*, they were saying to each other. *I just sent him a card the other day*, or, *I thought he was coming home. They said he would come home.* Yeah, I knew *exactly* what they were saying.

After a few moments, Millie broke off, poured a cup of coffee, and set it on the table for Dad. "I've got to call Jan, okay?"

We stared at the table, listening to Millie sob into the phone.

"Let's get out of here," Dad said, already climbing out of his chair, unbuttoning his shirt.

Jack stirred at the movement. "Where to?" I asked.

"I don't know." He wrested his air force shirt off. "But let's go."

chapter 17

We sat on the beach at Harveys Lake, sand crunching into our shorts because we didn't have a blanket or even towels. When we headed out, Dad just wanted to drive; we didn't know where we'd end up. At least he'd thought to change out of his air force clothes.

Jack lifted his nose in the air, sniffing different gusts. The fishy odor of the lake, the buttery popcorn scent from the concession stand, and the whiff of hot dogs breezed over us—a smorgasbord that smelled like summer.

Towels carpeted the beach. Brightly colored umbrellas looked like happy mushrooms sticking out of the sand. So many people laughing, playing, splashing in the water. Jack yanked at the leash. No sitting around for him.

"You want to go for a walk?" I asked.

He barked and jumped in answer.

"Dad?"

"Yep." He pushed himself up and dusted off his shorts. He always looked younger out of his uniform, especially in shorts and a T-shirt. Sometimes people thought he was my bachelor uncle instead of my dad.

As we walked, I kept Jack close by. We stuck to the loose, white sand, away from the actual shoreline so as not to bother people. Jack zigzagged on the leash like a divining rod—nothing was getting by him. He'd smell every smell on this beach before we left. I grinned, but when I looked up at Dad, I saw he was lost in thought.

"What are you thinking about?" I bet I knew.

He shrugged.

We passed a huge building with white letters on the roof: SANDY BEACH. Good thing they spelled it out for me—I never would've known. Jack snarfed up the ketchupy leftover of someone's hamburger without even stopping. His ears were erect, his step bouncy.

Dad sighed as we passed under the shade of the building. "I'll be going to the funeral."

I'd been to only one funeral, and I always tried not to think of it. Not to think of all the other ladies crying, not to think of the pastor who spoke but didn't really know my mom. Not to think of her body lying there with everyone staring at her. Her favorite flowers rested on top of her coffin. Dad had bought them. *She would have liked that*, everyone said. *No, she wouldn't*, I wanted to yell. *It means she's dead.*

When someone dies, it's weird because then there's a kind of party afterward. People eat and some drink beer and then they actually tell stories and laugh. *Laugh—w*hile you sit there knowing that even right now, a hoist is lowering your mother into the grave. A backhoe is pushing dirt over her. I swiped at my eyes. I must have gotten some sand in them. "I'll go with you," I said to Dad.

He didn't argue.

Jack pulled us along. Speedboats zipped out on the lake. The farther away we got from the building and paddle-boats, the less populated the beach became. The arches of my feet were getting sore from pushing through the sand.

Dad pointed to some patchy grass and a lone tree. "Let's sit over there."

We caught a bit of shade. Some high schoolers were out chicken-fighting in the water, the girls on top of the guys' shoulders tugging at each other and shrieking. Just as I leaned back to rub my foot, Jack took off.

I leaped up and ran. "Jack!"

He headed toward this boy and girl tossing a Frisbee. They didn't even seem to notice him.

"Jack!" Behind me, Dad whistled.

Then I saw—as if in slow motion—Jack spring up and catch the Frisbee. He trotted to me with the Frisbee in his mouth, the leash trailing behind him. But as I bent to grab it, he took off, stopped, and waited.

The boy laughed. "That was a good catch!" The girl was smiling, too.

I neared Jack. "C'mon, boy. Give me the Frisbee."

He huffed and planted his front paws in the sand, ready for takeoff. The boy and girl moved closer. Jack didn't move at all, but his eyes darted between the three of us.

"Gotcha!" The girl lunged for the Frisbee.

Jack hightailed it out of there, running right over the blanket of some adults.

"Dad, get him!" the girl yelled.

By now, my own dad had joined the chase. Jack bounced between us like a pinball in a machine. His eyes shone with excitement and his ears were red. Like a deer, he leaped and darted; there was no catching him.

Finally, their mom stood up with a sandwich. "C'mere, boy!" She waved it around. "C'mere!"

Jack's eyebrows lifted and crunched down as his gaze flitted over his pursuers. He took a halting step toward the lady, and she stretched her arm out with the sandwich. "Ham!" she called out to me, smiling.

Taking another step and then another, Jack inched closer until his nose was almost touching the bread. I moved slowly in. His nose twitched, being that close to the ham. He dropped the Frisbee and I snatched the leash.

"Yay!" The girl threw up her arms.

Their mom smiled at me. "Can I give him the sandwich?"

"Yeah, of course!"

She glanced over at Dad and me. "Y'all boys look hot. Whyn't you join us for some lemonade?"

Dad said, "No, no, we don't want to bother you. Thanks for helping us get the dog, though."

Waving him off, she pulled out paper cups and poured us some lemonade. "No bother a'tall."

Oh, man, that cold lemonade right then was the best thing I ever drank in my life.

She invited us to sit down and eat, so before Dad could protest again, I had my butt down and my hand on a plate. The boy and girl came over, asking if I was from around here. Their accent was about as strong as their mom's, and I was sorry to hear they were just visiting their grandma and heading back to North Carolina in a few days.

But, for a moment, as Dad and I sat eating their ham sandwiches and tangy potato salad, we were all in one spot, talking with our mouths full and laughing. There was no war here, nobody dying, no one being mean. We threw the Frisbee until we couldn't see it anymore. The sun turned orange and drifted behind the mountains, and everything became dark again.

chapter 18

I burrowed in the foxhole. Lying down, I couldn't see out and I hoped that meant no one could see in. "Well?" I asked Ray.

I heard his footsteps circle the fort and stop. "It's solid," he said. "I can't see in at all."

We'd worked on the fort almost every day and now we were finished. It was important that the fort blend in with the woods; we didn't want anyone discovering it. After digging out a burrow, we'd stuck big branches upright into the corners to serve as posts. We used Dad's tools to saw branches off trees and nail together parts of the walls. The gaps we filled with bushes and vines, weaving the brambles in good and tight and overlaying them with loose twigs and pine needles.

I climbed out of the fort so I could admire it again. From the outside, you could barely tell there was a fort there—it just looked like a patch in the woods. A covered trapdoor was the only way in. A pioneer couldn't have done better.

"This is going to be so cool," I said. I had plans for the fort. Ray and I would be the chiefs of a secret club with secret meetings. We'd induct frightened new members in the glow of our campfire. I inspected the fort thoughtfully. We'd need to build a chimney.

For now, we were going to play cards. Just as I lifted the trapdoor, Jack huffed and I heard a twig break. I snapped my head around and there was Prater, standing just a few feet behind us. The big, bad wolf. I faced him and dropped the trapdoor behind me.

He jerked his chin toward our fort. "What's that supposed to be?"

"Nothing," I said, but at the same time Ray answered as well.

"It's our fort."

I heaved my shoulders and blew out a big breath. "Ray!"

"What?" His face was innocent and relaxed. He really had no idea.

I moved quickly away from the fort to the blueberry bushes. I didn't want Prater looking at it. He might think he could be a member, too. "It's nothing. Just an idea we had. The real fort is going to be on top of the mountain. If we even build one."

Ray looked confused. I flashed my eyebrows at him and hoped he got my message.

"What's this, then?" Prater said. He stepped closer to the fort and pushed on the walls. Some of the pine needles tumbled down.

"Don't do that!" I snapped.

"I thought you said it wasn't anything," he said, his eyes narrowing. He pushed on it again.

I stepped closer to him. "It's not. Just leave it alone anyway."

"Yeah, Alan," Ray said. "Don't crush the walls; you'll ruin the fort."

"Ray!" I stared at him with my mouth open. What good was a camouflaged fort if he went around telling people about it—especially Prater.

"This is a fort?" Prater smirked. "It looks like a bunch of sticks first graders put together."

"Do you have to make fun of everything?" Ray said. "Besides, look how good it is." And before I could stop him, he opened the trapdoor and led Prater inside. Prater lumbered in like a bear for hibernation. I untied Jack and brought him into the fort with us, too.

We had to sit on the ground once we were inside. Ray and I did, anyway. Prater crouched as if ready to spring up if needed. I noticed his earlobe—it was misshapen. *From the dog attack.* I started to feel bad for Prater, but then he turned and made a sour face at me. "Do you have to bring that dog everywhere? I hope he doesn't pee in here."

My face heated up. "I hope *you* don't pee in here."

Prater rolled his eyes and curled his lip. He looked around the fort and gaped at the ceiling. "So what do you even do in here?"

Like I would really tell him. The deck of cards was in my back pocket. I shrugged my shoulders. "Lots of things."

"It's going to be a secret club," Ray said.

"Ray!" He was telling Prater everything.

"Yeah, right," Prater said. "A secret club. I saw it as soon as I came in the woods, so that's how secret your stupid fort is."

Ray looked irritated. "It's not stupid."

"If it's so stupid, why don't you just leave?" I said.

Prater leaned forward. "I didn't come to see you anyway." Then he turned to Ray. "I went to your house to see if you wanted to play basketball but your mom said you were here." He sneered at me. "It was easy to find you and your dumb fort, if you want to call it that. Just a bunch of sticks in a hole. How boring."

Ray started to say something, but I moved in quickly. "At least we did it ourselves. We didn't let Mommy and Daddy make us a little playhouse so we could play in it."

Prater frowned. "You better stop it."

"You better stop it," I said in a perfect imitation.

He glared at me. I stared back evenly. The worst he could do was punch me. I realized I'd rather get punched than back down from him. Finally, he shook his head and then looked at Ray. "If you want to come over later, don't bring him."

"Don't worry about it, I've got better things to do anyway," I said before Ray could even answer.

Prater slammed the trapdoor open and stormed out. "Air force brat!" he called out from the edge of the woods.

"Mama's boy!" I yelled from the trapdoor.

When I slipped back down in the fort, Ray had a strange look on his face. "What's wrong?" I asked.

He shook his head. "You and Alan."

My expression dropped. "What do you mean?"

"You guys make me feel like I have to pick one of you."

He was right, of course.

chapter 19

Dad was late coming home from work one night. I'd already eaten, scraping most of my supper into Jack's bowl. It was some kind of rice-and-corn tomato casserole that made me feel like puking. Jack seemed to love it.

Jack and I sat on the front porch steps as it grew dark. Usually when Dad was late, he called. The sky swirled with pink and purple, and the trees were stark black against it. I couldn't see through to the fort.

Crickets and frogs twanged their rubber band melody, and every now and then a lone bird called out. It was real peaceful. I slouched on the steps and closed my eyes. These were the sounds that used to lull Indians to sleep.

Suddenly, Jack yipped. I snapped to attention.

"What?" I didn't see anything, but I sure didn't want Prater to take me by surprise again. "What is it, Jack?"

Then I heard it, a faint howl lifting to the moon, followed by another. Prickles rushed over my head and the back of my neck. I held on to Jack, who had become rigid.

"That didn't sound like a dog," I said. One look at Jack's face told me he agreed. Even in the evening light, I could see the blush seeping into his ears and eyes. His body tensed, ready for action. He stood and curved his skinny tail over his back.

The howl echoed from deep on the mountain once again. Jack leaped against my arms, but I held him tight. Shifting and prancing, he struggled against me, huffing in frustration.

"No, Jack!" I yelled. I grabbed his leash and he dug in with his front paws, pulling and pushing his neck in the collar, almost slipping out of it. I threw my arms around his body and he bucked me off, but not before I got ahold of his collar. He jerked hard down the stairs and we tumbled to the bottom. Before he could scramble away, I wrapped my legs and free arm around him, pinning him like a wrestler.

Then we heard it again, a howl rising out of the mountain. I froze. Even Jack was still. Seconds went by, then minutes; then all was quiet again. It didn't matter. I recognized the sound from every cowboy movie I'd ever seen. It was a coyote.

I put Jack in the house. I grabbed my tape recorder, set it on the porch, and pushed the button to record.

In a book I once read, some pioneers came across a ghost town in the desert. All the houses were still standing and even had furniture in them, but there were no people. The pioneers decided to leave their wagons and sleep in the empty beds of the empty houses. By morning, coyotes had eaten all of them and they were now just skeletons lying in beds.

I was still waiting on the front porch when Dad pulled into the driveway. I sprang up and ran down the driveway to the car, ready to burst with news of the coyote.

"Hey, kiddo," Dad said as he stepped out of the car. His uniform looked rumpled, like it had been a long day.

The car shone under the porch light. I tried to brush away some dirt clods from the back end, but then I realized they were dings. The whole quarter panel was pocked. "What happened to the car?" I asked. It looked like it had been through a meteor shower.

Dad's smile faded into his tired face. "Well." He sighed and shook his head.

I waited for him to finish.

Dad wiped his face with his hand and let his shoulders drop. "Some people threw rocks at it."

"What?"

Dad sighed again and fingered one of the dings as if to smooth it out. "I stopped by a job fair today. Some protesters were there." He smiled at me, but it was that kind of upside-down smile people use to show you they're not upset about something they really are upset about. "People are not happy about the war." He rubbed his eyes. "They need someone to blame."

The air force insignia shone out from the driver's door like a target. My chest tightened. "They threw rocks at it? Did you see them?" They'd drop their rocks and protest signs if they saw my dad coming after them.

Dad looked at me. He stood there in his wrinkled air force uniform next to his bashed-up air force car. "I was driving the car when they did it."

My eyes widened and I stared at him. My dad. How could people do that to him? He was a good man. It wasn't his fault there was a war going on—he was just doing his job.

"It's all right," Dad said gently and cupped my head.

"No, it's not." I shook off his hand. "They should be arrested." How dare they do that to my dad.

"Joshua . . ." He nudged me gently toward the house, but I stood my ground.

"Did you stop? Did you get out of the car? What did you do?" I spat my words, I was so mad at those people.

He hung his head. "It's not like that, it—"

"You let them get away with it?"

"Joshua . . ." His bones seemed to melt, as if something had sucked all the marrow out. Then he turned toward the back door. "I'm going in."

I stared after the crumpled figure of my father. What was happening to people? Why were they acting this way? It made me afraid of becoming an adult. They seemed so full of hate. I did not want to be a person like that.

Dad stopped on the back porch. "You coming?"

I thought about telling him about the coyote, about the tape recorder on the front porch, but his shoulders were sagging under the weight of his day. I didn't think I should add anything else.

"Yeah, I'm coming." I trudged up behind him.

As I lay in bed that night, I imagined myself tracking down the people who threw rocks at my father. They said they didn't want war but then they opened fire on my dad. That sounded like war to me.

chapter 20

Sound crackled and popped, and a high-pitched note blared from the microphone as Pastor Danny stepped up to the podium. Jack whined, and I covered my ears like everyone else. Just about the whole town turned out for the Fourth of July Family Festival.

"Happy Independence Day!" Pastor Danny said over the PA system. "Glen Myers is over there getting seconds on the ribs and I told my wife I'd better say the blessing."

Laughter rose from the tables. "Better hurry!" said an older man standing near the buffet with a plate.

After the laughter died down, the pastor's face took on a shine. "Before we say grace, I want to deliver some good news." He smiled off to his side and gestured with his hand. A guy, college-age, got up and stood next to him. A few days' whiskers covered his cheeks.

A shriek went up from the crowd, then everyone around us broke into applause. The guy bowed his head and pushed his hand against his eyes before looking up again.

The pastor stretched his arm across the guy's shoulders. Then he faced us. "Folks, Mark Zimmerman is home safe from Vietnam!"

Shouts and whooping filled the air. Dad stood up and clapped, and so did several other men, and finally, everyone got to their feet. The pastor joined in, then motioned for people to sit down.

He leaned up to the microphone. "Mark, we are so happy to have you home. I know I'm speaking for your family, especially your mom, when I say a day didn't pass without prayers being said for you."

Mark shut his eyes and nodded.

"We're proud of you. We love you. And we thank you for what you did in the name of this country." The pastor stepped aside. "You want to give us a few words?"

Mark gripped both sides of the podium. Applause and victory shouts greeted him. He turned his back and pressed his hand against his eyes again. When he faced us, head down, silence fell in the tent.

"Thank you for . . ." His voice crumbled. I willed my strength to him. After a few moments, he picked up his head and looked at us straight on. "Thank you for welcoming me back. Thank you for being kind to my mom and dad while I was away. I can honestly say not every guy coming back from

'Nam comes back to a picnic." He stared at us like he was going to say something else; instead, he broke down again.

A man and a lady rushed up. The lady was crying.

"Ah, Mom." They hugged each other, and the father wrapped his arms around both of them.

Then the soldier squared himself up. "All right, no more tears. I've got a few people to thank; I hope you're all here. Tyskos, the magazines you sent me got passed around till the pages fell out. Millie Thompson, best chocolate chip cookies ever, next to my mom's. Pastor, ladies of the church, Mom and Dad, all your letters, all your prayers . . ."

"We love you, Mark!"

Looking out at all the people sitting in front of him, he didn't seem to know where to go from there. He took a deep breath and glanced at the pastor.

Pastor Danny took the podium, gave the blessing, and then it was all the ribs, corn on the cob, and baked beans you could eat. Barbecue smoke drifted under the canopy, reminding you of how good it all tasted and making you want to eat more. I shared some ribs with Jack as Dad and I sat at a picnic table.

Something fluttered through the back of my hair. I swatted at it and kept eating. Again, a definite ruffle, then giggling. I reached back real quick and grabbed a little hand. "Gotcha!"

"Joshua!" CeeCee squealed. She whirled around and sat on the bench next to me.

Dad leaned backward. "Who've we got here?"

"I'm CeeCee!" She faced Dad with her pumpkin smile, swinging her legs back and forth. Then she bent under the table. "Hi, Jack!"

Jack sniffed and licked her hands. How could she be so cute and her brother be such a jerk?

"What are you up to?" I asked. And more important, "Is your brother here?"

"Yeah, he's over there." She pointed off in some direction.

I spotted Mr. and Mrs. Nichols, Mrs. Puchalski, and a couple of kids from Sunday school. One kid waved to me and I waved back. I didn't see Prater. I put my head down when one of the mothers from the ice cream store walked by.

"Guess what?"

"What?"

She tipped her face up. "I have a dog, too."

"What?" This was news to me. "I didn't see a dog at your house."

She dropped her shoulders exaggeratedly like I should know better. "Not a *real* dog—a *doll* dog. He's pink. There's Missy!" She popped off the bench and disappeared.

Other people brought their dogs—real ones—but Jack didn't enjoy meeting them. He jerked himself away when they sniffed him, and he yapped at their snouts if they got too close to his face. I knew exactly how he felt.

My plate empty and my stomach full, I held my fingers under the table and Jack licked them clean. I gathered up his leash and turned to Dad. "I'm going to find Ray," I said.

Jack and I wove through tables and clusters of people until I spotted him.

Ray smiled when he saw us and pointed at Jack. "Look at his mustache!" A ring of barbecue sauce framed Jack's lips. We laughed and sat at an empty picnic table at the edge of the pavilion.

"Prater's here," I said. I wondered why he wasn't hanging around Ray.

"Yeah, I know." Ray kicked at the dirt. A black spider scurried off. "He's mad at me."

"Why?"

Ray shrugged his shoulders.

A truck hauled up and some kid and his mom got out.

"Jimmy Schwartz," Ray said.

A couple of boys ran out to greet him and his face grew serious as he spoke to them. Whatever he said, it wasn't good, judging by the shocked expressions he received in response. His mom split off to talk with the ladies. The boys stopped by us.

Jimmy had red hair and greenish freckles. He nodded to Ray. One of the other boys elbowed Jimmy and said, "Tell him what happened."

I leaned forward. I saw Prater coming up out of the corner of my eye. The other boys acknowledged him with a nod as he sat at the picnic table across from us. I did not look at him.

"Some kind of fox or something broke into the chicken coop and killed a whole bunch of chickens," Jimmy said.

He stepped over the bench and sat down, hunching his shoulders as he leaned on his elbows. "When we ran outside, most of the chickens were lying around bleeding. He ate a couple of them, too." His face screwed up. "Dad had to kill the others; they were too hurt for living."

"Were the chickens screeching?" Ray asked. "Is that why you ran outside?"

"No, we heard the trash cans banging around and—"

"Trash cans?" Prater asked and moved to our picnic table. My heart quickened. Trouble.

"Yeah, we heard them getting knocked down or something. Then we—"

Prater pointed at me. "His dog knocks down trash cans."

They all turned in my direction and their eyes fell to Jack, who sat beside me.

"He didn't knock down any trash cans," I said. "Nobody actually saw him do that."

"Yeah, and remember at the ice cream store?" Prater said, his voice getting louder. Other kids were gathering. "He killed that rabbit. We *all* saw him do that, even you," he sneered.

My mouth went dry. Prater seemed to be enjoying this.

"I heard he chopped it right in half," one kid said. A couple of other kids nodded.

"That's not what happened," I said. I stood up and gripped Jack's leash.

"Jack didn't do anything wrong," Ray said. "Even cats hunt."

"But that's mice," a girl said.

"Speaking of hunting," Prater said. His eyes lit up with excitement and his mouth dropped open. Suddenly I knew what he was going to say. I stepped over the bench and backed away from the table.

"That dog is a hunter," Prater said, then pointed at me. "He got a letter that says so. That dog is trained to bring *meat* to the table."

"No," I said, shaking my head. "Jack didn't do anything."

"Of course you'd lie for him."

"I'm not lying." I couldn't bear all those faces looking at me and Jack like we were criminals.

"Hey, Jimmy," Prater yelled. "Why did you say it was a fox?"

Jimmy looked bewildered. "We saw these paw prints—"

Prater flashed me a triumphant grin.

I ducked away from the table, pulling Jack into the crowd. Ray called me, but I didn't stop. Prater was the biggest idiot on the planet. He was trying to get everyone to gang up on me and Jack; that wasn't fair. Ignoring Prater didn't work because he was *looking* for a fight. I let myself say a cussword, but only loud enough for my own ears to hear. It didn't make me feel better. The only thing that would make me feel better was getting out of here.

chapter 21

I reined Jack in close and tripped through the crowd until I spotted Dad, leaning his crossed arms on a picnic table. Mark Zimmerman hunched over the other side. He was looking down while he talked, but I could tell it was an intense conversation.

Normally, I wouldn't interrupt Dad, and even now I reconsidered it, but all I could think of was shaking this place. I jerked Dad's arm hard.

"Hey!" He smiled up at me. "Mark, I want you to meet my boy. This is Joshua."

"How're you doing?" Mark said. He looked younger up close.

I gave him a quick nod. "Dad, come on. Let's go."

"In a few minutes. I'm talking right now."

I groaned.

I could see him trying to figure me out, but I didn't feel like explaining right then. I just wanted him to get up.

"Let me have a few minutes with Mark."

I threw my head down. "I'll be by the car."

I had plenty of time to think while waiting for Dad. Like, why didn't I stick up better for Jack? Why didn't I tell them about the coyote? I hadn't heard it since that night, and my cassette player hadn't picked up anything, but I knew this like I knew Jack's bark—a coyote roamed somewhere on that mountain and he was coming down to hunt.

I whiffed on that. I should've told them. Instead, at the height of trouble, I froze—I hated that about myself. Now, of course, I could think of all kinds of great comebacks, but it was too late for that; the moment had already passed. How dare they blame Jack for those chickens.

And Prater. What a complete—

"You want to tell me where the fire is?" Dad came tromping through the field. "You were disrespectful not only to me but also to a soldier who just got home."

"I didn't mean to be."

"Well, you were. Next time hold your horses when I tell you to."

"Yessir."

We piled into the car.

"So you gonna tell me what's going on?" Dad asked as we drove home.

"I just—they're blaming Jack for everything," I said. I

told him what happened to Jimmy's chickens and how Prater had twisted everything.

"Well . . . ," Dad began. He took a deep breath and exhaled slowly. "Is there anything else you want to tell me?"

"Like what? What do you mean?" I turned and faced him as we slowed to a stop for a red light.

Dad stared out the windshield. "Didn't you take Jack for a walk this morning?"

"Yes," I said slowly, unsure of where this was going.

"Did Jack get loose?"

"No!"

"You can tell me if he did."

"You don't believe me! You believe them!"

Dad raised his hand, waving it like a stop sign. "No, no, no—I'm just saying that . . ." He paused and sighed again. "I'm just saying that maybe we should keep a better eye on Jack."

"Jack didn't hurt those chickens. There's a coyote on the mountain. I heard it with my own ears."

"A coyote?" Dad lifted his eyebrows and shook his head. "This isn't the Wild West, Joshua. I know you love Jack and you want him to be innocent, but you can't make up stories to protect him."

"I knew it!" I said. "I knew you wouldn't believe me. You think I'm lying!" I folded my arms and glared out the window.

"Stop," Dad said with a sharp voice. "Maybe you think you heard something, and maybe you did. But last month you told me you saw a bear up there." I didn't turn from the window. He softened his voice. "I think you're letting your imagination run away with you."

I twisted around and looked at Jack in the backseat. His head stuck out of the window and his eyes squinted against the wind. His nose twitched like crazy. He looked even more golden with the sun lighting up his fur.

Turning back, I looked straight at Dad. "He didn't do anything," I said. "He's a good dog."

chapter 22

Ray called about an hour after we got home. I picked up on the upstairs phone and dragged the handset into my room. He was saying I should've stayed at the picnic table. "In a couple of minutes, they would've all forgotten about it. But when you left, everyone was all like, 'Yeah, it was his dog—that's why he's leaving.' I had to stick up for you all by myself."

I hadn't thought about that. "Well, if it hadn't been for Prater—"

"He's a blowhard, man, everyone knows that."

Even though he couldn't see me, I shook my head. "They believed him." It had been like being encircled by the enemy, with Jack and me at the center.

"I don't think Jimmy did. Anyway, you missed my yo-yo routine."

"Oh, man." Some friend I was. Silence buzzed over the wire. "You know what? I'm an idiot. I should have told Prater to shut up."

"Not that he would have listened." Ray laughed. "Maybe I could have done a looping trick and popped him in the head with my yo-yo."

First he called Prater a blowhard, now he was popping him in the head with a yo-yo. Something was up. "Remember you said he was mad at you? What was it for?"

"I showed him the arrowhead!" His voice raised, full of disbelief. "I told him we could probably find one for him, but he got all mad about it. He thinks I can only have one best friend."

Best friend. Words of gold to a new kid. I had to be careful here, didn't want to say the wrong thing. I just kept my mouth shut.

Ray sighed into the phone.

I pictured him yo-yoing. "How'd your routine go?"

"Great! My new trick—that one where I jump over the string—it was so cool. They blasted the music so loud, it was like a concert!" He paused for a second. "Are you still going to the fireworks at Harveys Lake? We're all going to Hanson's Park afterward. You *have* to go on the roller coaster."

I'd already told Dad I didn't want to go. "Who's all going?" I asked.

"Everyone! Come on, you can't stay home."

Yeah, I could. *Everyone* included those kids who'd looked

at Jack as if he were a monster. *Everyone* included the ice cream ladies. *Everyone* included Prater.

"My dad's kind of busy."

"We can pick you up."

"No," I said quickly. "I—I . . . I think Jack's a little sick from all that barbecue sauce. I'm just going to stay home." Maybe sit on the porch and listen for that coyote.

Then I said, "Hey . . . um . . . have you heard anything weird at night, like up in the woods or anything?" I tried to make it sound like it wasn't any big deal. I wasn't even sure if the sound could carry to the houses off the mountain. Ours was pretty high up.

"What do you mean? Like . . . ghosts?" He laughed.

"No, not like that." I gazed out my window. "The other night I heard—Jack and I both heard—oh, you won't believe me, never mind."

"Tell me," Ray insisted. "I *will* believe you."

I bunched up the cord in my hand and let it spring out. "We heard a coyote."

"No way!" Ray said. "A coyote?"

I knew it. I shouldn't have said anything.

"Yeah." My voice trailed down. I heard how stupid it sounded. I cringed as I imagined Ray's face filled with disbelief. He'd hang up and call Prater and they'd both laugh at me.

"What does your dad say?" Ray asked.

"He doesn't believe me."

Silence. Then Ray said, "I've never seen one around here."

"Well, I heard it. I heard it howling. It doesn't matter anyway; no one believes me," I said. "Everyone wants to blame Jack."

"You really heard a coyote?"

"Yes," I said firmly.

There was a moment of silence. I knew Ray was trying to decide if he believed me or not. It didn't matter; I was prepared to face the rest of summer alone with Jack.

"Do you think that's what attacked Schwartz's chickens?"

He believed me. Before I could answer, he went on. "Oh, man, you should've heard what Jimmy said after you left—that coyote really tore into those chickens. I sure wouldn't want to run into one."

Hearing him talk about it made it even more real. Relief and determination rushed through me. I told him everything about the night Jack and I heard the coyote, how it made my hair stand on end. "No one else believes me, but I'm going to prove it."

"How?"

I glanced at the tape recorder sitting on my nightstand.

chapter 23

An unfamiliar car sat in our driveway one night when Jack and I came back from our run.

It was Mark Zimmerman's. He and Dad sat at the kitchen table, their heads bent in deep conversation.

"Hey," I said, hanging up Jack's leash.

"Hey, kiddo," Dad said. "You remember Mark?"

"Yep." Jack zipped by me to the living room. I wanted to follow him, but I didn't want to be rude again. I leaned against a chair. "How's it going?"

"Pretty good."

They both stared at me like they were waiting.

Oh. "Well, nice seeing you."

In the living room, I checked out the newspaper comics, but bits and pieces from the other room kept my ears pricking.

"... and my dad thinks I should be pounding the pavement ... don't want a job in a factory ... people giving me dirty looks ..."

I knew how that felt. People crossed the street when they saw me and Jack coming.

Mark described his dreams, horrible nightmares that woke him up in cold sweats. "Can't talk to my old man about it—he delivers bread, for crying out loud."

"What about your friends?"

I couldn't hear his response.

If you didn't have friends, you sank. That was the biggest pitfall to always moving. You were constantly starting over, making the same moves again and again ... watching ... waiting.

I leaned over and gave Jack such a good roughing up that he bounced off the couch and sprang to the floor, head lowered, front legs splayed.

"You want to play?"

He huffed.

I whipped his rope toy across the room and watched him bound after it. Dropping it at my feet, he settled back and waited for me to throw it again. One thing about Jack, you always knew what he wanted. I tossed it a couple more times, but he got wise fast and was already running before I threw it, so I faked him out and threw it into the kitchen and heard a crash.

"Joshua!"

Jack ran out of there with his tail between his legs. I felt the same way as I slunk into the kitchen, where I spotted Millie's cookbooks all over the floor.

Dad tipped his head at me. "Could you be more careful?"

Heat flashed through my face. Getting yelled at in front of Mark made me feel like a little kid. I bent down to pick up the books.

"What kind of dog is he?" Mark asked.

I shuffled Millie's books back onto the counter. "He's a Pharaoh hound."

Mark pursed his lips in thought. "I've never heard of that."

"It's a rare breed," Dad said. I caught a note of pride in his voice. He looked at me hesitantly. "Joshua, maybe you should—"

"No, no." Mark pushed his chair back. "I've taken up enough of your time." He stood, nodded, and shook Dad's hand. "Thanks for talking to me, man. It's been hard getting my head together."

"Anytime." Dad clapped Mark's shoulder and opened the door for him. "You come by anytime, okay?"

After he left, I asked, "Is everything all right?"

Dad rested heavily against the cupboard. "Yeah."

Whatever it was, it was between them. Dad wasn't about to spill.

chapter 24

"I didn't hear anything," Ray said.

We sat in my room listening to the recording from the previous night. Jack lay dozing in a warm spot by the window. The sunlight bounced off him, creating a golden halo around his body.

"Me either." It was the third night in a row that I'd left the cassette player recording on the porch before I'd gone to bed. Howling was what I hoped to hear, but static was the only thing that played from the cassette.

The tape ended and we sat back.

"Maybe we need longer tapes. Like a couple of hours' long," Ray said.

I nodded. A couple of hours into the night would definitely be better than the half-hour tapes I had now.

"Tysko's has them," Ray said. "We could get some today."

I rewound the tape. "I don't have enough money, and I can't ask my dad." If he didn't believe there was a coyote, he definitely wouldn't give me money to try to record it.

"I've got some," Ray said. "We could pool our cash together."

"I thought you were saving up for that new yo-yo."

"Yeah," he said, shrugging his shoulders, "but I don't want Jack to be blamed either."

I knew then that Ray was a solid friend.

I opened the drawer where I kept my money and jammed the bills and coins into my pocket. "Let's go," I said. At that, Jack rose. Anywhere I went, he went, too.

"Millie, we're going to Tysko's," I shouted through the open basement doorway as we passed to the back door. I could hear the washer and dryer humming.

"Okay," she called up.

After Ray grabbed his money, we left our bikes at his house and walked with Jack across the street to Tysko's. The doors stood open, and a dust devil blew across the wide plank floors. We walked past the breads to get to the shelf of batteries and cassettes, but old Mrs. Tysko came around the corner and blocked the aisle.

She put her hands on her hips. "What do you boys need?" she asked. She looked mad.

"Cassettes," Ray said.

She looked at Jack and me and then pointed to Ray. "*You* may shop." Then she looked at me and arched an eyebrow. "That dog is not welcome here."

"Jack's okay," Ray said and touched Jack's head.

She kept her eyes on me. I felt like a criminal. "I know all about that dog." She pointed to the doorway. "You can come here alone, but that dog is not welcome in the store or in the ice cream area outside."

Ray began to protest, but I said, "It's okay. We'll wait outside." I didn't want to stay in there with her anyway.

"*This* time you can wait outside," Mrs. Tysko said. "But don't ever bring that dog to my property again."

"C'mon, Jack," I said. We walked out, sat on the wooden steps, and I rested my chin in my hands. It was so unfair. After a few minutes, Ray came outside with the cassettes. He looked apologetic. "Wasn't your fault," I said, getting up.

He sighed. "Yeah, I know, but still . . ."

Jack hunted that rabbit and now people wanted to charge him with everything. I stood and stretched. Then I remembered what my dad said about the war and people being unhappy about things. I said, "They just need someone to blame. That's why we need to get that coyote on tape."

We rode home slowly and zigzagged up the hill. As we got closer to the house, Jack started barking, but even Ray and I could hear the thrashing in the woods. I threw my bike down without letting go of Jack's leash and tore into the woods. Ray ran behind us.

"Hey!" I yelled through the trees.

Branches snapped close by but the sound grew farther and I slowed down by the blueberry bushes.

Then I saw it.

chapter 25

The fort was wrecked. Someone or something had bashed in the walls and knocked down the posts. The branches lay broken, sticking in the hole like kindling. The trapdoor was cracked in half.

Ray's shoulders slumped. "Geez," he murmured.

I felt sick as I looked at the destruction. "It was such a good fort," I said.

"Yeah," Ray said. He began to pull branches from the heap. Then he stopped. "I don't think we can fix it." He was right; it was obliterated. I tied up Jack and dragged myself to the ruins.

"Maybe we could just use the hole," I said, "like, for campfires and stuff."

Ray considered the idea. "Yeah, that would be good."

But not nearly as good as having a fort. Ray and I had

worked hard on this one. We'd nailed a plank up high for squirrels to run across, and even that had been destroyed.

Anger burned in my heart. "I don't think an animal did this."

Ray examined the debris and tapped a branch against his leg. "I don't think so either."

Neither of us said anything after that. It was hard work, stooping over the hole and heaving the logs out. Prickers were in the brambles we'd scattered over the roof; I grabbed a pile of branches and got stuck by one.

"Ow!" I said and dropped the pile. Blood trickled from little pinpoints on my hands.

"You okay?" Ray asked.

"Just some prickers," I said and wiped my hands on my shorts. As I bent down to pick up the pile again, I saw a flat, odd-looking piece in the brambles. I shook it loose from the other twigs and branches and held it in my hands—a leather strap etched with the figure of a horse. Drops of my own blood stained it.

"Prater!" I snarled. My lips tightened and I squeezed my hands into fists.

Ray stopped. "What?"

I slapped the wristband into his hand.

He straightened up, giving a curt laugh. "Alan," he said. "I can't believe he wrecked our fort."

"I can! He's a mean, stupid idiot!" I picked up a stick and

hurled it through the woods. "I know he's your cousin, but—"

"He shouldn't get away with this." Ray looked mad.

Something unleashed inside of me. I stomped over to Ray and snatched the wristband from him. "He's not going to." I went over and untied Jack.

Ray followed me. "What are you going to do?"

Energy pumped through me. My heart was hard as a rock. "He wrecked our fort—I'm going to wreck his."

"No," Ray said. "That won't solve anything."

"Yes, it will. We'll be even." Prater would know what it felt like. Stupid wristband. But when I looked at it, really looked at it, I thought it was cool. If I had one of Jack, I'd wear it, too. The wristband wasn't stupid—Prater was. I wanted to go over there with a shovel and fling horse manure all over his stupid dressed-up little tree house.

"Let's go talk to him." Ray crossed his arms. "See what he has to say."

Talk? That's not what I had in mind. But I could sure think of a few choice things to say.

chapter 26

As Ray, Jack, and I made our way up Prater's driveway, I heard the muffled report of a rifle—target shooting. We leaned our bikes against a corral post, and I held Jack's leash tightly as we climbed the hill to Prater's tree house.

Just as he'd described before, the tree house sat on a platform in the split of the tree trunks. A log staircase led up to a small cabin with a shingled roof and a wide-planked door, which stood open.

Jack and I jogged up the steps behind Ray to the doorway. I'd seen forts and tree houses before but never anything like this. A braided rug covered most of the floor. Two rocking chairs sat together in the far corner, like they were just waiting for people to sit down and talk. Pictures of Prater and Shadow filled the walls. There was even a little table. It looked more like a place for CeeCee to have tea with her dolls than a place for boys to hang out.

Prater sat on a bench holding a rifle, the barrel resting through the window, another gun on the floor. His face was pink and sweaty—no doubt from running all the way home after trashing our fort. He'd obviously heard us tromping up the stairs because he didn't act surprised to see us, and he didn't say hello, not even to Ray. Then he saw Jack. His knuckles whitened as he clutched the gun, then he turned so red I thought his head would explode. "What do *you* want?" he snarled.

"Alan—," Ray started.

"You wrecked our fort!" I blurted.

"Your *fort*?" he sneered. "Your dog probably got loose and smashed it. Or maybe the wind knocked it down."

My voice dripped with contempt. "The wind?"

Prater shrugged. He laid down the gun, stood, and his mouth twisted into an ugly smirk. "Could've been a bear."

"Oh, yeah?" I said, thrusting myself forward. I shook the wristband in his face. "Do bears wear these?" He tried to grab it, but I whipped it behind my back. "You liar! You wrecked our fort."

"Give me that wristband," he growled.

"Not till you admit you wrecked our fort."

"You better give that back to me."

"Or what?" I was suddenly reminded of when he snatched my letter from the dog club.

He shoved me hard on the shoulder. I stumbled backward, almost falling over the bench. Jack rushed at Prater, snapping, snarling, and gnashing his teeth. Prater tried to step away, but Jack checked his every movement. Fear flashed in Prater's eyes. A thrill swept through my body; I'd never seen Jack like this before. My heart swelled with pride that he was protecting me, even though it was scary at the same time.

"Jack," I murmured. "It's all right." But Jack did not give up his position. Prater was pressed against the wall of the tree house. I crouched beside Jack and smoothed his fur. "C'mon, boy, it's okay." I drew him closer to me.

Prater peeled himself off the wall. "That dog almost bit me! I should call the police on him."

"Come on, Alan," Ray said. "You started it."

"So what?" Prater said indignantly. "He could've attacked me and *you* don't even care!"

"Oh, my God." Ray stared at him.

For a second, Prater looked hurt. Then he remembered himself and glared at me. "Get out of my tree house."

"What about our fort?" I said. "We all know you did it."

"I DON'T CARE ABOUT YOUR STUPID FORT. Give me my wristband!" He lunged at me, windmilling his arms.

Jack leaped and barked. His lips pulled back to reveal sharp, white teeth. A scissor bite. "You better watch it," I said, reining Jack in and moving toward the doorway. I turned and whipped the wristband across the room.

"No," Prater yelled, "*you* better watch it—you and your stupid dog." He bent down, but instead of grabbing the wristband, he grabbed a gun, raised it to his shoulder, and aimed it at Jack.

The hairs on my arm stood up and I froze. I felt blood whoosh through me. Prater held the gun steady, head tilted, one eye shut, the other eye focused with hate. I couldn't breathe. I did not blink.

"Put that down!" Ray yelled. "What's the matter with you?"

Prater shifted his fingers and gripped the gun firmly. "I want them out of here." He cocked the hammer.

My heart dropped. Blood drained from my face. I sensed Ray at my side and Jack by my legs, but all I could see was the end of that barrel. I stepped in front of Jack.

"I'm getting your dad!" Ray took one step toward the door and stopped.

Prater held the gun steady. I swallowed.

Jack growled a low warning. Outside, two birds called back and forth to each other, and a breeze rustled through the leaves. Prater opened both eyes and lifted his head. He lowered the gun to his side. "It's just a BB gun," he sneered, "and it's not even loaded."

My heart beat light and fast, and my lungs pumped quickly as though I'd been running. Heat crept into my face. "You're an idiot," I said to Prater in a low voice.

"You're a wuss."

I wanted to hit him.

"Come on, Jack." My legs felt shaky as I climbed down the stairs. Jack sensed my lack of balance and slowed down. My eyes stung, but I wasn't going to let Prater think I was crying.

"Josh, wait," Ray said, leaning out of the doorway.

I shook my head without turning around. All I wanted to do was get out of there, but I walked to show Prater I wasn't afraid of him. I wasn't a wuss.

"Joshua!" Ray called from the tree house. I looked up to him. He had one foot on the steps and one foot in the tree house. He stared at me and Jack for a second, then he pressed his lips together and turned to Prater. "Sometimes you *are* an idiot," he said. He bounded down the steps and caught up to us. "Come on, let's go."

Prater rushed to the doorway. "Hey, Ray!"

Ray kept walking.

"You're not my cousin anymore," Prater spat.

"Who cares!" Ray shouted without turning around.

We mounted our bikes and flew down the driveway with Jack sprinting alongside. Just before we hit the first curve, I looked behind us. Prater stood leaning against the bottom of the tree house steps; he had the BB gun trained on us. I mashed down on the pedals.

chapter 27

Later that night, I sat alone in front of the TV without watching. I was still mad about this afternoon. Prater and his stupid wristband. I should never have given it back to him after what he did. The phone rang in the other room, and I heard Dad pick it up. After a few seconds, he raised his voice and sounded angry. I wished people would leave him alone about the air force. My thoughts drifted back to Prater and his guns. He probably pictured himself as a gunslinger—or a *cowboy* with his horses.

I heard Dad put the phone down hard. He came into the living room and he didn't look happy.

"Joshua." He snapped off the television and sat on the chair next to the couch. Leaning forward, he pressed his right fist into his other hand. "I just got off the phone with Bruce Prater."

My back shot up ramrod straight.

"He says you threatened his son—"

"*What?*"

"You sicced the dog on Alan."

"No way! He's lying! He pulled a *gun* on me!" My whole body tightened. I rushed into the story about the fort and finding the wristband and going over there to confront Prater. "He pushed me, so Jack growled at him, that's what happened."

Dad stared at me. "And then he pointed the BB gun at Jack."

My mouth half-open, I nodded quickly.

Lines appeared on Dad's forehead. "Why didn't you tell me this earlier?"

I blinked rapidly. I couldn't believe Prater told his dad. I hadn't told *my* dad because I didn't want more trouble with Prater. "Well, it wasn't loaded or anything."

"For all you knew, it *was* loaded. That kid has no right threatening you like that." He rose from the chair.

"What are you going to do?" My voice pitched higher than normal.

"I'm going to call his father and let him know what really happened."

"No!" When he looked at me, I said, "Don't—it'll just make things worse between Prater and me." I stared at him until his posture relaxed and I knew he'd changed his mind.

"I don't like letting this go," he said. "Even a BB gun can

158

hurt someone. Is there anything else I should know? Is that all that happened?"

"Yes, sir."

He took a deep breath and exhaled slowly. "Did you know Alan was mauled by a dog when he was little?"

I nodded.

"That dog almost killed him. Bruce said Alan was in bad shape for a while." He shook his head. "He also said he might file a report, but I think I talked him out of it."

My eyes bulged in their sockets. "Jack didn't do anything! Prater was the one. He pushed me. He's had it in for us ever since we moved here. Jack was protecting me."

"Yes, but—"

"Isn't that why we got him? To protect me?" I shouted.

Dad's jaw tensed. He shifted in the chair. "It's not really working out the way I thought it would." Before I could protest, Dad held up a hand to stop me. "Look, we've had a lot of trouble with Jack. If anything else happens . . ." He shook his head.

"What?" I said, fear flowing in my blood. "If anything else happens, what?"

Dad looked at me with a sad expression.

"No!" I roared. "We're not giving Jack away."

"Joshua—"

"No!" I yelled as I bounded up the stairs. Jack galloped behind me.

I slammed the door and fell onto the bed. Jack hopped

up and licked my cheek. Everything was closing in on me. The only safe place was with Jack. I lay there, my thoughts racing, until I heard a car roll up our driveway. My heart struck a hard beat. Prater's dad couldn't have called someone already.

I jumped to the window and saw a guy getting out of his car. The tightness in my chest eased up. It was just Mark.

"Don't worry, boy," I said as I turned from the window to Jack. "I won't let anything happen to you."

chapter 28

It's weird how cemeteries are actually nice places, if you don't count the gravestones. The smell of fresh-cut grass breezed over the grounds. Huge trees cast pools of shade over the sloping lawns. I shivered against the morning chill, but already the sun touched my arms, a promise of the heat to come.

I stood next to my dad in the cemetery. He wore his crisp dress uniform. Army, air force, and marine veterans—young guys and old-timers—mixed in with a crush of people from town. I spotted Mark in his dress blues. He looked different somehow. It wasn't just the uniform; he carried himself differently. While the rest of the people his age bent their heads to talk or slouched with their hands in their pockets, Mark faced forward, eyes level, hands at his sides, his back ramrod straight. I fixed up my posture.

So many people turned out for David Kowalski's burial that the crowd curved around the open grave, a dark hole with boards and lashes laid over it. Dad and I somehow ended up sort of facing the family. I tried not to, but my eyes kept returning to them. Is that how Dad and I had looked? Skin sagging off our faces, eyes dim, unseeing? The lady I pegged as the mother sat shrunken into herself. I looked away from her.

As a bugler played "Amazing Grace," army soldiers marched to the hearse and hefted out the coffin. Mrs. Kowalski's shoulders started to shake. She pressed a tissue to her mouth. A man, her husband, laid his hand on her arm.

They had played "Amazing Grace" at Mom's funeral, too. She picked it out herself. Picked out her own dress to be buried in. Told Dad what prayers she wanted for the service. Everyone said she looked like she was sleeping, but I didn't think so. That body in her coffin didn't look like her; it looked like a statue of her.

I flexed the muscles in my jaw and faced David Kowalski's casket.

When the preacher got done talking, the army pall-bearers stepped up and folded the flag. They had white gloves on, and the last guy to hold the flag pulled it to his chest like he was hugging it.

Mrs. Kowalski groaned and shook her head as he walked up to her with it. "No, no, no . . ." Her husband wrapped his arm around her. Together, they took the folded flag from the soldier. She clutched it now in her lap, rocking. The girls behind me let out little sobs.

Dad and Mark and the other veterans held their salute.

Off to the side, I heard, "Ready!" and the cocking of guns. Seven army soldiers held their rifles. "Aim!" A silence. "Fire!"

Boom! I flinched big-time. Seven military-issue rifles firing at the same time . . . it was a sound that commanded my whole body to attention. As a group, they fired two more times—a twenty-one-gun salute. Then a bugler played "Taps." I could see houses across from the cemetery. Could they hear the bugler? Did they sit in their kitchen listening to those lonely notes and wonder *Who's being buried today?* I would not want to live in any of those houses.

When it was all over, people went up to the family; some got in their cars. Mark shook hands with the father and said a few words to the mother; then he came over and joined us.

"You shaved!" I said. He'd gotten a haircut, too.

He gave me a sharp nod. Military mode, I recognized it immediately.

Dad asked, "How are you holding up?"

Mark looked straight at him. "He was two years ahead of me in school. I can't—" He clenched his jaw, swallowed.

I watched Dad watch Mark, and I saw him make a decision. "You wouldn't mind taking Joshua home for me, would you?"

"No, sir."

"But, Dad!" My response came automatically. I didn't know why. It wasn't like I wanted to stay at the graveyard or talk to the family, and Jack was probably busting to get outside anyway. It made me feel better to think of Jack. "Okay, never mind."

As Mark and I climbed into his Mustang, I saw Dad shake Mr. Kowalski's hand and grip his shoulder. Then we took off.

"Cool car," I said, rolling down the window.

"Thanks, I got it before." *Before Vietnam.*

I stuck out my hand and let the wind push it up and down.

"Man, that was heavy." Mark had his sunglasses on, but his voice gave him away.

"Were you guys friends?" That's the hardest thing, if it's someone you know, someone you care about. I didn't know David Kowalski.

Mark shook his head. "Didn't know him that well." His chest rose with a big sigh. "But some of my friends—" He swallowed noisily a couple of times before going on. "Guys I met over there, they bought it. They died. My sergeant was only twenty-one. . . ."

"My mom was thirty-two."

He glanced at me, then looked back at the road. "Man, I'm sorry. I just—I don't know—how do you get over it?"

I felt that familiar sting at the back of my eyes. "You don't get over it," I said slowly. Mom was still alive in movies I kept in my head. I thought about her every day. "You never

164

get over it. You just . . ." I didn't know how to explain it, so I used Dad's words. "You learn to live with knowing they're gone."

We rode ahead, both of us lost in our own thoughts. The valley was farm after farm with black-and-white cows and old barns. We passed by rows of corn and straw-colored patches of land. The wind carried the sweet field scent into the car along with the heat.

"You want a Coke or something?" Mark asked. "I'm dying of thirst."

"Me, too."

As Mark paid for our drinks at a drugstore, a guy and a girl got in line behind us.

"Hey, G.I. Joe!" The guy snorted. The girl giggled, covering her mouth.

Mark pocketed his change and handed me my drink.

"Did you have fun in Vietnam?" the guy said. "Did you kill any babies?"

I looked at him with horror, then at Mark. Mark's eyes hardened, but the only thing he said was, "Come on, Joshua."

My mouth dropped as he pushed open the door and walked out. I couldn't believe he wasn't going to do anything. Just as I was about to follow him, I heard the guy inside snort.

"Big tough guy," he said. The girl punched his arm and told him to stop, but she laughed.

I gritted my teeth and stood back in the doorway. My neck and face burned with anger. "Shut up," I said.

The guy tilted his head like maybe he didn't hear me right.

"Shut up!" I said again.

The girl raised a hand to her mouth.

The guy put his stuff down on the counter and sauntered over. My eyes narrowed. I squared my shoulders. He stood almost as tall as Dad but looked about Mark's age. When he planted himself in front of me, he said, "Your buddy's a killer—you know that, right?"

I stared at him hard.

Behind me, the bells jingled and the door opened. The guy startled.

"Joshua." It was Mark.

The lady at the counter backed up. "I don't want any trouble in here," she said, but it was Mark she looked at.

"There's no trouble here, ma'am," Mark said, then he directed himself to the guy. Their eyes locked for a moment.

The guy didn't say anything. Mark gave one sharp nod, then turned to leave. As he pushed through the door, the guy's body relaxed.

I pierced him with my eyes. "Big tough guy," I said.

When we got into the Mustang, Mark wedged his Coke bottle against the cigarette lighter and flipped off the cap. He tilted the bottle up and drained about half of it before starting the car.

I popped mine off, too, but I held it at my side. "Why

didn't you say anything to him?" I asked. "Why didn't you do something?"

He cranked the wheel and took us out of the parking lot, onto the freeway. Wind whipped through the car as he accelerated. Staring straight ahead, he answered, "I won't disgrace the uniform."

chapter 29

Every night, I set up the tape recorder, and every morning I listened to the cassettes. Sometimes Ray came over and we'd bend our heads close to the speaker, trying to hear something—anything—but so far, nothing. Even with the longer tapes, I was only getting an hour and a half or so each time, and it was about the same slice each night.

I started setting my alarm for five o'clock in the morning to insert a new tape and then I'd go back to bed. Most mornings, I'd fall right back to sleep, but Friday morning I felt restless. Jack's legs sprawled across the bed and I couldn't get comfortable. I tried lying on my side, my back, my stomach, but finally, I got up and changed into my clothes.

Dad was just leaving as I went downstairs. I hadn't forgotten what he said the other day about getting rid of Jack if anything else happened. Inside, I felt mad at him for that—he knew Jack; he liked Jack. How could he even think about giving him away? But I couldn't let on my feelings without reminding Dad about it, so I got my breakfast and tried to act like everything was normal between us. Maybe he'd forget what he said about Jack.

After he left, I felt fidgety; I needed to get out of the house. I left a note for Millie, then hooked up Jack and got on my bike. "Let's go to Ray's," I said. Jack didn't care where we were going; he just loved to be outside running. He looked like a racehorse, slicing through the wind.

After we rounded the curve to Ray's, I spotted a police car and a bunch of people standing outside the house before Ray's. That old lady's house. Maybe she died or something.

As we got closer, I saw Ray and waved. A look of horror crossed his face when he saw me and he made weird gestures I didn't understand. I heard sobbing and hysterical wailing.

"That's him!" someone shrieked, and that's when I saw her, Mrs. Brenner, pointing at Jack. Her hair was wild and her eyes looked crazy. She wore a housecoat. "That's the dog!"

I felt like someone had punched me in the gut.

"Now, hold on a minute, Mrs. Brenner," the police officer said, holding her arm.

As the policeman tried to calm the old lady down, Ray cut through the crowd to me. "Something killed her cat," he said quietly. He puckered his face. "It was all shredded apart on her sidewalk."

Before he could continue, the old lady shuffled up to me

with the policeman right behind her. She shook her finger at Jack.

"I saw him," she hissed. "I saw his yella eyes glowing. I saw his bushy tail—"

"His tail's not bushy!" I yelled.

The policeman looked at Jack's wire-thin tail. "You sure this is the same dog?"

"I saw him!" she insisted.

"Son, where was your dog early this morning?"

Just then a car screeched to a stop.

All heads turned as Dad got out of the car and strode up the sidewalk. I felt proud and relieved as I watched him walk up in his sharp, blue air force uniform, with its ribbons and stripes. They wouldn't gang up on me now.

Dad acknowledged me with a sharp nod. "Joshua," he said. He was in air force mode. He looked at the policeman. "What's going on here, Ed?"

The policeman sighed. "Another attack on small game." He shook his head.

"I'll tell you what's going on!" the old lady yelled. "That devil dog killed my cat." Tears ran down her face. "I saw him my own self. I went to get the newspaper and saw him—" She broke off, sobbing.

The policeman shook his head. "I'm sorry, but I got to ask you this, Rich. Was the dog out this morning?"

Dad didn't even pretend to be friendly. "My boy and his dog were eating Pop-Tarts half an hour ago."

"And the dog was in the house all morning." It was a question, but the policeman made it sound like a statement.

"Ed, this is ridiculous."

"I know, I know, I'm just doing my job here, Rich."

Dad glanced upward and sighed. "Look, Joshua and Jack were just getting up when I left a little while ago."

The policeman nodded his head. "Okay, then."

"Joshua, get in the car," Dad said.

"You're letting them go?" the old lady shrieked.

"Joshua," Dad said firmly. "Get in the car."

"I'll come over later," Ray said quickly.

I got into the backseat with Jack as Dad loaded my bike into the trunk. Dad settled in behind the wheel, but before we could leave, the policeman walked up to Dad's open window.

"Hey, Rich, no hard feelings, okay? Just doing my job. A lot of talk's been going around about your dog, but her description and the timing don't work out."

"That's 'cause Jack didn't do it," I yelled from the backseat.

"Joshua," Dad warned.

I grabbed the back of Dad's seat and pulled myself forward. "You should look up on the mountain—there's a coyote up there." I said. Good. Now the police knew. Maybe they would do something about it.

But instead of concern, a look of doubt crossed the officer's face. "Son, I've heard a lot of things about your dog. I'd advise you to not go around making up stories." He turned to Dad and tapped the top of the car. "Sorry, Rich."

Dad gave him a quick nod and drove home. He didn't say one word the whole way. This was going to be bad.

chapter 30

"What were you thinking?" Dad yelled once we were home in the kitchen. Millie decided to make herself scarce in the basement with laundry or something.

"You don't go spouting off to a policeman like that." He wiped his palm across his face and stared at me. "I'm not sure we can keep Jack anymore."

"What?" My heart pounded. My mouth went dry.

"He was supposed to be a fun watchdog—instead, he's terrorizing our neighbors."

"Dad!" My insides wrenched, and my gut filled with a wild, anxious feeling. "Even the policeman said Jack didn't do it."

"*This* time," Dad said. "But there's been other trouble. I can't have our neighbors coming after us like an angry mob."

"But you said that if anything else happened, *then* you'd do something. This wasn't Jack. This doesn't count."

Dad stared at the floor for a long time. I wanted to shout for Jack's innocence, but I knew I'd already made my point. Better to not push it. I looked at him, waiting for his judgment.

"Okay," Dad said. "I'm late for work." He mustered himself together, picking up his briefcase, the reason he'd come back in the first place. "One more chance, Joshua. That's all," he said. "I can't keep bailing Jack out of trouble."

A few minutes after Dad left, someone tapped the glass on the back door. After all that had just happened, I was afraid of who it could be—the policeman, that old lady, maybe even Prater.

I ignored the tapping and hid out on the stairs, but Jack leaped away from me, barking. Whoever it was, Jack wanted them to know they'd have to get past him first.

The rapping came louder.

"Joshua," Millie called from upstairs. "Can you get that? I'm ironing."

Oh, man. There goes my cover. I sauntered to the door, prepared to face trouble.

Instead, it was a friendly face.

"Hey, Mark," I said. "Dad's not here."

"I know." He shoved his hands in his pockets. The muscles in his arms flexed, and I noticed for the first time his left bicep sported a tattoo of an eagle holding olive branches.

"I was coming out of Tysko's when I saw all the commotion. Just wanted to make sure you were okay, little man."

"I'm okay, but . . ." I didn't know how much I wanted to tell him. Whose side would he be on? "Did you see that cat?"

He nodded. "I've seen worse." Jack jumped up and down, pawing Mark at the chest. Mark held his hands out to pet Jack.

I measured him, taking in his open expression, the eagle tattoo, his hair, which was getting scruffy again. He was okay, I decided. Even Jack thought so.

"Um . . . you want to come in?"

"Sure."

We hung around in the living room, throwing Jack's rope as we talked. I told him what happened, including all the stuff that happened before, like Prater when we first moved here and the Fourth of July. I even told him about the coyote.

Mark drummed his fingers on the side table. "Maybe you should try to catch it."

"I'm trying, but the tape recorder's not picking up anything."

"I mean actually catch it—trap it."

Okay, that got my attention. "How would I do that?"

"Trip wire would do it. Maybe a pit."

"But he would jump out."

"No, you put metal spikes in it."

"That would kill him!"

Mark looked at me. "Yeah, no one likes killing." Settling

back into the cushions, he closed his eyes and rubbed his forehead. His body seemed to sink into the couch.

"Mark?" I asked quietly. "What was the war like?"

"Mmm, don't want to talk about it."

"You talk about it with my dad."

He put his hand down and glanced at me plainly. "Your dad . . . he's easy to talk to."

I thought about how I had tried to explain the trash cans and chickens and Jack to Dad and how he didn't care. "Maybe for you."

"Maybe for you, too, little man. Give him a chance."

I thought about that for a second, too, but then I remembered something. "How come you don't talk to *your* father about the stuff you and Dad talk about?"

Mark's mouth flattened into a line. "My old man . . . he dropped out of school and took a job to help his mother when his father died. He's still driving that same bread truck." He laughed with disbelief. "Just because I don't want the same kind of life he settled for, he says I think I'm too good for it. And it's not that.

"It's just . . . it's hard for me to be *here* when I know what's going on over *there*." Mark leaned forward and looked directly at me. "Some guys didn't make it back—I *did*. I can't just drive a bread truck. What he doesn't understand is that I feel like I've got to do something more important, something bigger."

"Like what?"

"I don't know." He sank back into the cushions. "I just want to make a difference."

I stared at him, trying to think of how he could make a difference. Become a doctor, maybe, or a pastor. Firemen, they help people.

After Mark left, I thought about the traps he mentioned. Spikes nailing the coyote in the chest. Paws sliced up. I pushed those thoughts out of my mind. All I wanted to do was clear Jack's name. That old lady, Mrs. Brenner, almost had the policeman believing Jack had killed her cat. If it hadn't been for Dad pulling up at the right moment, I wasn't sure what would have happened. Anyway, Ray said he would be over later, and he'd fill me in on everything.

chapter 31

I was sitting on the back stoop watching Millie hang laundry out to dry when Ray finally skidded into our driveway. He was practically bursting with news, so we ducked inside, out of Millie's earshot.

"She was trying to say it was Jack. She didn't know his name, just kept going on about the devil dog."

"I told that policeman there was a coyote up there." I whipped Jack's rope across the living room. He galloped after it.

Ray looked hopeful. "What'd he say?"

"That I was making up stories." I shook my head. "Dad says we have to get rid of Jack if anything else happens."

"What?" Ray's eyebrows shot up.

I looked at him and nodded.

"Maybe you could just keep him home all the time."

"He was home this morning and still got blamed," I pointed out.

"Maybe I could go with you whenever you go out, and I could be a witness that he didn't do anything."

"No," I said. "They'd think you were lying, too."

"What about the tapes? Have you listened to the morning tapes?"

"Yeah." I shook my head. "Nothing."

We fell into silence.

Millie came in, set the basket down, and served us each a piece of pecan pie. Then she grabbed her purse. "I'm going out for groceries," she said. "Chicken, ham, some things to get you and your dad through the weekend. You boys stick around here, okay?"

No problem there. I wasn't exactly eager to set foot in town today. My thoughts went from the groceries to the policeman saying "small game" when my gaze settled on the laundry basket.

Suddenly I got the idea for the perfect trap. "We're going to catch that coyote," I said to Ray.

He put his fork down. "How?"

"Well, he eats chicken and cats. We'll leave some out for him."

Ray looked horrified. "You mean tie a cat up outside?"

"No!" I said. And then I unfolded the beauty of my plan. "We'll put Millie's chicken in the trash can."

Ray gasped with understanding. "Yeah, put it in the trash can and leave the lid off so he can really smell it."

"When he knocks it down, I'll hear it and run outside and—" And what? It wasn't like I could grab him with my bare hands.

"Maybe you could . . ."

This was going to be harder than I thought. On TV, they always put the bait under a little cage held up by a stick. When the animal went for the bait, they pulled the stick out and the animal was trapped. The laundry basket wouldn't hold a coyote. Neither would an overturned trash can.

I shook my head, resigned. "No one's going to believe us unless they see him."

Ray thought for a second. "What about your camera?"

My heart quickened. "Yes! That's it!" A picture was undeniable proof.

With the camera as our weapon, the plan quickly fell into place. After Dad was in bed, I would sneak out and put the chicken in the trash cans. I'd leave the lids partly on; that way, they'd still let the smell out, but they'd also make a lot of noise when the coyote knocked them down. I'd leave the camera on my windowsill; since my windows overlooked that side, I could shoot the picture from there and have instant proof.

Ray and I sat back, full and satisfied. Our plan could not fail.

chapter 32

Except it did.

Mark came over that night. Dad invited him to stay for supper, but he stayed a lot longer than that. Normally, I didn't mind when Mark stopped by—he joked around with me and played with Jack—but his being here tonight threw off my schedule. I wanted Dad to be in bed while I set about baiting the coyote.

Instead, we had pizza delivered and knocked back a few root beers.

"Old enough to fight, not old enough to drink," Mark said, raising his bottle to Dad; then he finished it off.

Dad chuckled.

"Well," I said. I smacked the couch cushions and stood. Mark was done. This night was over. But no, they just sat there and looked at me. I walked over to the front door and leaned on it.

"Joshua?" Dad tilted his head at me.

Peeling myself off the door, I strode between them to the kitchen. It was almost ten. "Is he ever going to leave?" I asked Jack. He followed me back into the living room, where I scooped up his rope toy and sat on the arm of the couch.

Blah, blah, blah. They kept talking. I thought about when Dad and I drove to Harveys Lake and that lady baited Jack with a ham sandwich. How much more would a hungry coyote go for chicken drumsticks?

"Joshua!" Dad leaned over and jerked the hem of my shirt. "Sit down. You're making me nervous. Either throw that thing or quit fiddling with it."

I'd been slapping Jack's toy against my other palm. Jack stood at the ready. Unlike me, he was very patient. I tossed it for him and slumped down onto the couch.

Dad asked Mark, "Did you look over those papers I gave you?"

"Yep."

"What papers?" I asked. "You're not reenlisting, are you?" I'd heard about guys going back.

"No." Mark gave his head a quick shake. Then a grin took over his face and he said, "I'm going to college."

"I've been talking to Mark about using his GI benefits. He's thinking about Penn State."

Everyone talked about Penn State. "But that's not even close to here," I said.

Mark shrugged. He didn't know what I was talking about.

"You just got back. Don't you want to stick around for a while?" If I was from somewhere, I'd be glad to be back. You wouldn't see me taking off right away.

"It's only two hours away," he said. Then to Dad, "I can come back whenever my laundry pile gets too high."

They laughed.

"Yes, sir, I like that idea a lot. So does my old man."

I said, "I thought your dad wanted you to deliver bread like him."

Mark tapped his hand against the armrest. "Yeah, but then your dad here talked to him. Convinced him that going to college would get me a lot further than a bread truck ever could."

"That's right," Dad said.

Mark grinned. "But when you told him the service would *pay* for college, that sealed the deal."

I remembered what Mark had said about wanting to make a difference. "What are you going to study?"

"I don't know yet."

"That's okay," Dad said. "You'll figure it out. You've got your whole life in front of you now."

"Yep," Mark said, his face turning serious.

It felt like he was going to spend his whole life *here*

tonight. I rubbed the tops of my legs and patted out a rhythm. I sent mental messages to Mark: *Time to go home; time to go home. Go home so Dad will go to bed and I can bait the trash can.*

They were still talking when I got up and wandered into the kitchen. Opening the fridge, I saw Millie's chicken in a big container, just waiting for me. First, I'd—

"What're you poking around in there for?" Dad yelled from the living room. "There's more pizza out here."

I rolled my head upward and shut the fridge door.

Oh, man! Back in the living room, I saw they'd started on the second pizza.

"Jack needs to go outside," I muttered. Jack's ears pricked at the word "outside." He sprang and darted around me, almost blocking my way to the back door.

"Don't go too far," Dad said. "It's late."

I reached for Jack's leash and hooked it onto his collar. "Yeah, it *is* late," I said, then Jack and I slipped out the door.

The night air chilled the backs of my arms. Tiny emissions of light sparked against the darkness, fireflies threading their way through the trees. Except for Jack's excited snuffling, it was dead quiet out here. He tugged toward the woods, but there was no way I was heading up the mountain in this blackness. I pulled him away, and we jogged down the hill.

The coyote had struck this morning. I wondered where it was now. Maybe it watched me from deep within the woods. *No*, I thought, *Jack would know. Jack would smell him.* Still, a shiver zipped through my spine. I felt like a soldier in the bush.

After we reached Mrs. Puchalski's house, we turned around for home. Mark's car was still in the driveway. Once inside, I unhooked Jack and he rambled into the living room to greet them. I sighed heavily as I hung up Jack's leash.

"I'm going upstairs," I said, skulking through the living room.

Dad looked up. "All right, kiddo." Talk about oblivious.

"See you later," Mark said.

I shut my door on them.

chapter 33

It had been nearly a week since I came up with my plan, but every single night got messed up. Twice, I fell asleep before Dad did. Once, I set the alarm, but that set Jack off and Dad woke up.

Mark was becoming a regular visitor. I wandered into the living room after supper one night when Dad had to take a phone call, leaving me alone with Mark.

"Hey, little man. What've you been up to?" Mark stretched his legs out.

"You're kind of here a lot." Oh, man. I couldn't believe I said that. I watched his face for insult, but he nodded.

"My dad told me the same thing."

I sat down on the opposite end of the couch. "Why *are* you here so much?"

He took a deep breath and exhaled slowly. "Remember

when you first moved here and you felt like everyone hated you?"

"Yeah . . ."

"And even though you'd seen some stuff, you couldn't get anyone to understand you?"

"Yeah . . ."

"Well"—he glanced off to the side—"that's how I feel."

"But you're *from* here!" I erupted.

He shook his head. "Not anymore. I just . . . Everyone expects me to be the same as I was before. I'm not." He drew his eyebrows together. "I mean, I'm still me, but I've got this whole other thing now, you know? And nobody wants me to have it."

I didn't know what to say.

"Except your dad. He knows."

And then I realized there are some bonds that are sacred. Like the bonds between soldiers. Between families. Between Jack and me.

Bonds that cannot be broken.

Only I could protect Jack. It came down to me. He was more loyal than any friend I'd ever had, and he trusted me. Prater, that policeman, even Dad—they were against Jack. But he was innocent and I knew it. I would capture that coyote on film and deliver the true enemy.

Waiting out Dad that night was hard. I tried to read, but my head kept dropping with sleep. Jack slept at my feet; he had no hint of the mission that lay before me.

At midnight, I slunk out of bed, careful not to disturb Jack. I crept into the hallway and padded my way through the dark, quiet house to the kitchen. When I threw open the refrigerator door, there was the chicken, wrapped up in aluminum foil. I took it out and went through the back door, closing it gently.

The midnight air was cool, and a chill shuddered right through me. I crept around the house to the trash cans. Earlier, I'd positioned them for the perfect camera angle. Now it was time to load the bait. I unwrapped the chicken, and the delicious smell of garlic and spices rose up. My stomach gnawed at me—I'd pretended I wasn't hungry at supper because I wanted to leave as much chicken as possible for the trap.

I broke off a drumstick and smeared the inside of both trash cans and lids with it, making sure they got good and greasy. Then I broke the meat apart and put some in both cans and left the lids teetering on the rims. Yeah, when those fell down there would be plenty of noise. I looked up to my window. Perfect.

I slipped back inside, washed up, and slid into bed with no one the wiser.

chapter 34

Jack and I ran down a grassy hill, kicking up dandelions as we ran. Fuzzy white bits floated and drifted in the breeze and I laughed. Suddenly Mrs. Puchalski ran down the hill banging her pot lids. Jack turned and barked ferociously at her.

I woke up. Jack was really barking and I heard the clatter of trash cans. My heart almost leaped through my chest. I tore to the window just in time to see two furry creatures feasting on the chicken. Raccoons.

I threw the window open. "Hey!" I yelled. Jack stood with his front paws on the windowsill, barking excitedly. The raccoons looked up at us; they held our gaze for a moment as if deciding how bad the threat was. Then they took off.

My bedroom light blinked on. "What's going on in here?" Dad asked. His hair was ruffled and his eyes were half-shut.

"Aw, just some raccoons raiding the trash cans." I shook my head and tried to act annoyed. "We scared them away."

Dad walked over to me and patted my shoulder. "Scared me, too." He glanced out the window, then pulled it shut. "You hop back in bed now. See you in the morning," he said, snapping off my light as he left.

I felt bad as I listened to him walk back to his room. I'd sort of lied to him and it made me feel guilty. He trusted me; I was planning to betray his trust. And yet I had to. For Jack.

I gave Dad a few minutes to fall asleep, then got out of bed to reset the trap. Jack dropped softly to the floor, and his nails clicked on the wood as he followed me.

"No, Jack," I whispered and crouched beside him. "Stay here. I have to go by myself."

I got up, turned away, and heard him clicking after me.

"Jack—" It was useless. Excitement colored his eyes. His ears blushed and stood erect. Something was up and he knew it.

"Okay," I said. "But you have to be quiet."

We slipped through the house like shadows and made our way to the refrigerator. I looked at that ham. Through the plastic, I could see the pineapple rings crisped with brown sugar. Cloves decorated the crisscrosses Millie had sliced across the meat. I licked my lips. Dad would kill me.

The chicken was already gone—that would take some explaining. But I didn't think I'd be able to explain the disappearance of the ham *and* the chicken. I shifted around the cheese and found some bacon and bologna.

I closed the fridge. Jack sniffed the air, raising himself for a moment on his hind legs. He licked his chops.

He followed me to the back door. "No, no, Jack." I couldn't bait the trap and hold him at the same time.

I backed up to the door and twisted the lock and the handle. Cool air breezed through the crack. With my back against the door, I pulled out a few pieces of bologna and threw them deep into the kitchen.

"There you go!" I said. He went after it like a chowhound, and I slid through the door and pulled it shut.

The trash cans lay on their sides. I looked at the chicken left behind by the raccoons. It wasn't much but, together with the lunch meat, it might be enough to draw a coyote.

The bacon was raw and greasy. I smeared it all over the outside of both trash cans and then the insides before throwing it in with the bologna. The garlic aroma of the chicken wafted up, mixing with the bacon and bologna, and altogether it smelled like a trashy deli. A smell that—I hoped—would be irresistible to coyotes.

Jack greeted me at the door, inspecting my hands. He licked the grease and trotted away. I washed my hands.

The trap was set. We went back to my room and waited.

chapter 35

My light was out and I lay in bed with Jack beside me. My senses were on high alert. Blood surged through my body and my muscles tensed, ready to spring at a moment's notice. My eyes could make out every detail of my darkened room, and I could clearly see the picture of me and Jack on my nightstand. My ears picked up sounds beyond Jack's light breathing: the occasional groan of the house as the wind shifted, the rattle of the living room screen downstairs, and the hum of the refrigerator.

I fell into a black, dreamless sleep.

Suddenly I was awake, heart hammering, Jack barking and jumping. The metallic clang of trash cans resounded from the driveway. I flew to the window and looked down.

Coyote.

His fur was dark and thick, and his tail was a bushy bottle brush drooping behind him. He was about the same size as Jack but heavier. He tore at the chicken.

My legs weakened even as a jittery energy raced through my veins.

"Dad!" I fumbled with the camera. The first shot didn't go off. "Dad!" Jack thrashed at the window and barked violently.

The second shot fired off and the coyote jerked his head up. He froze for a moment and I saw his yellow eyes piercing through the darkness. In that liquid yellow gaze, I saw all that he had done, all that Jack was being blamed for.

I bolted from my room with Jack at my heels. We rushed past Dad, who was just now coming out of his room, still numb from sleep.

"What?" he mumbled. "What are you—"

"Coyote!" I yelled from the stairs. I raced to the back door and flung it open just in time to see the coyote cut through the woods. Jack bounded over the steps and charged after it.

"Jack!" I shouted. The anger I felt toward the coyote now turned into dread for Jack. I tore barefoot through the woods after him.

I followed the sound of breaking branches and the drumming of Jack's footsteps. We headed in the direction of Prater's but at a sharply lower angle, taking us to one of the streets that ran parallel to ours behind the woods.

Jack sailed over a chain-link fence. Barking and high-pitched yipping erupted. I ran up to the fence and climbed over into the yard, my eyes scouring the dark lawn. No coyote. Just a little white dog on a back porch yipping at Jack and trembling. Jack ran along the fence, agitated and confused. He growled and whined and shook off my hand when I tried to calm him.

A porch light snapped on and flooded the backyard. My eyes darted to every corner—no coyote. I heard the door being unlocked, and a gray-haired man with a white T-shirt and a big belly yelled from behind his screen door.

"Who's there?" His voice was deep and gravelly.

"Um . . . I am." My voice quavered. "Joshua Reed."

"Who?" The man pushed open his screen door and squinted at me.

"I—my dog—" I stammered. "He was chasing a—"

"Raccoon," Dad said. He jogged up to the fence, but by his breathing I could tell he'd been running at breakneck speed.

I shook my head at Dad. "Not a raccoon—"

"Joshua, grab Jack." Dad turned to the old man. "Raccoons have been dumping our trash cans. The dog had to go to the bathroom and took off after one."

The old man scowled. "Need to control your dog better."

"Yes, sir," Dad said. "I'm sorry about the disturbance."

The old man frowned, scooped up his dog, and disappeared back into his house, turning the light off.

I grabbed Jack's collar and led him out through the gate.

Dad gripped my arm as we came out. "More trouble? After our last talk?" he growled. "Did you think I was joking?"

I spun and faced him. "I got his picture!"

"What?" Dad snapped, confused.

"I took a picture of the coyote. Now you'll see." I had to walk bent over since I didn't have Jack's leash and I couldn't let go of his collar. "He was in our trash cans—I set a trap— didn't you hear it? Didn't you hear Jack barking? I kept calling you."

Dad glowered at me. "I didn't hear anything."

"Wait till you see the picture. Wait till everyone sees it." Jack would be proven innocent and everyone would be sorry.

When we got home, I rushed upstairs to get the picture. There it sat on the windowsill, the evidence of Jack's innocence. As I walked to the window, I heard Dad come into the room behind me.

I picked up the picture and stared at it. My insides crashed. It was a perfect picture—a perfect picture of the window frame and screen, nothing but darkness behind it.

"I knew it!" Dad thundered over my shoulder. He ripped the picture out of my hand and spoke to me through clenched teeth. "Nothing! Just your wild stories."

"But, Dad—"

"I've had enough," he said hoarsely, flinging the picture to the floor. "Go to bed." His face hardened. "No more sneaking around."

My eyes widened in protest. "I wasn't—"

"Enough." He slammed my door shut behind him.

chapter 36

When I woke up the next morning, my heart jolted with one thought: *coyote*. He was real, and I'd seen him. I peeled the covers off and looked at the picture I'd shot last night. As hard as I stared, I could not make out the coyote's form in the darkness beyond the window. But he was there. I knew it. Now I had to prove it.

Flashes of Dad's anger filled my mind. How he'd yelled at me, how he didn't believe me, how he'd slammed the door. If only he'd woken up sooner, he'd have seen that coyote for himself. I shook my head. It didn't matter. The coyote would be back. And I'd be waiting for him.

I was still staring at the picture when my door opened and Dad stepped in.

"It's late," he said.

I nodded, looking at him.

"Get dressed. Eat breakfast."

"Okay," I mumbled.

"You're grounded."

"What?" I couldn't be grounded—I had too much to do. I had to get more bait. I wanted to look for tracks. I needed Ray to come by and go over the whole thing bit by bit with me to make a better plan for tonight. "I can't be grounded. Not today."

Dad shook his head. "Joshua, you do not have a choice in this. You snuck out of the house last night."

"I didn't sneak out. I called and called you, but you—"

Dad held up his hand and closed his eyes. "Enough. I don't want to hear it again." He looked at me and his jaws tightened. "You're grounded for the weekend. No going out of the house and no one coming over. That's it." He turned and slipped out of the room. "Get dressed," he called from the stairs, "and eat your breakfast."

I tried to keep out of Dad's way after breakfast. I didn't want him any angrier than he already was. Jack and I looked at my shoe box stuff for a while, and I read some comic books. Voices floated upstairs, Dad's and Mark's and someone else's. I figured having company might have helped Dad cool down, so I took a chance and went downstairs.

"Hey!" Mark greeted me. He seemed looser than usual, lighter. "What's going on?"

If we'd been alone, I could've told him all that happened last night. I bet *he'd* believe me, and he might even help me. But Dad was here and this other man. "Nothing," I said.

"So you're Joshua," the other man said, his eyes crinkling with a smile. "I'm Mark's dad." He stuck out his hand. For a second, I thought he was doing that thing adults sometimes do—shaking kids' hands because they think it's cute—but he didn't have that jokey look on his face. I was a real person to him.

I shook his hand.

He clapped me on the shoulder. "Your father's a fine man. I hope you haven't minded sharing him with Mark." Then he turned to Dad. "Thanks again for all you've done. If there's ever anything we can do for you, let us know."

Before Mark followed him out the door, he stopped and shook Dad's hand, too. "Thanks, man. You've been great." To me, he said, "See you around, little man."

Dad smiled. "Keep in touch."

Mark's hair had been growing out since the funeral. I watched him walk behind his dad in his jeans and T-shirt. It struck me all of a sudden how young he looked.

"Mark!" I called before he made it to the car. "How old are you?"

"Nineteen!" He gave me a big smile, then waved and piled into the car.

"Are they going somewhere?" I asked after they left. Those were pretty big good-byes.

Dad allowed himself a grin. "They stopped by to tell me Mark's registered for college. Not Penn State—too late for that—but he'll be starting at the community college this fall."

So that's why he was smiling. "That means you'll still see him."

"It means"—Dad paused—"he's going to do something with his life. He's going to have all kinds of opportunities." Dad's face was open, his voice upbeat. "I feel like—I feel like it's me going to college!"

I high-fived him. "Way to go, Dad!"

He was no good at holding it in—he broke into a big, wide smile. Afterward, he futzed around the house, fixing things, cleaning, even humming as he worked. He was the happiest I'd seen him since we moved here.

chapter 37

Later, in my room, I studied the photo I'd taken, hoping desperately to make out some part of the coyote. Being grounded kept me from talking to Ray, but maybe I could think it through by writing a letter to Scott. I grabbed a pencil and a notebook, but when it came down to it, I didn't feel like writing a letter; I felt like taking action.

Suddenly, I heard a car roar into the driveway, screech to a stop, and *Wham! Wham!* Two doors slamming shut. Loud banging at the back door. I heard people yelling, and one sounded like a kid. I jumped up to my window and saw a police car pulling in behind a truck. I shot down the stairs. Jack ran with me, barking the whole way.

Dad beat me to the door. I stepped behind him as he swung it open. Prater's dad filled the doorway with his huge frame.

Dad moved squarely in front of him. "What's going on here? What's this all about?" he shouted over the yelling.

Mr. Prater's face was red. "Your dog—your dog—"

Ed, the policeman, leaned in front of Mr. Prater. "Listen, Rich, there was an incident at Bruce's place this morning. I was called in—"

"Incident?" Mr. Prater yelled. "That dog killed my boy's horse."

My heart dropped. I caught a glimpse of Prater behind his dad. His eyes looked swollen and the rims were red. Dried streaks of salt stained his cheeks and his whole face was puffy. He cried openly.

Stricken, I stood behind Dad.

"This dog didn't do anything," Dad said.

"First he attacks my kid, then he—"

Dad stepped forward. "Back off, Bruce," he said in a low, menacing voice I'd never heard before. "You're on my property."

"Yes," Ed said, turning to Mr. Prater. "I told you before to let me handle this. Step back from the door."

Mr. Prater glared at Dad. Taking one step back, he shook his finger at Ed. "You'd *better* handle this." The veins in his neck popped out. "You'd better do something this time."

Ed took a big breath and exhaled loudly. "Something attacked their horse early this morning. Got ahold of its hind leg and ripped it up something good. Tore into some of the muscle and buttocks, too. Bruce ran out, fired a shot in the air, and saw a dog run into the woods.

"The vet came out but said there was too much damage. They had to put the horse down."

On those words, sobs shook Prater's body. Poor, gentle Shadow. That beautiful horse. I felt tears spring to my own eyes. I knew how I'd feel if something hurt Jack.

"Your dog did it," Prater said, trying to control his sobs. "I know it was him."

I shook my head, scared. "Jack's been home all morning."

The policeman waved his notebook. "We got a witness found your dog loose in his yard early this morning."

My mouth dropped open. I stared up at Dad.

"Yes, the dog got loose." Dad folded his arms.

My breath escaped me. I couldn't believe Dad would betray me like this.

Dad narrowed his eyes and tilted his head. "What else? What real proof do you have?"

Ed stared at him. "Well, the animal that ran away headed into the woods in your general direction."

"You mean he ran into the woods."

Ed sighed. "Okay, I can see where this is going." He turned toward Mr. Prater and his voice became clipped. "Bruce, do you have a definite description?"

Mr. Prater's face bulged with rage. "I had a horse to take care of," he said between clenched teeth. "Are you going to let him get away with this? I don't believe it! He destroys our horse and you're letting him off?"

"Mr. Prater, go to your truck," Ed said.

"What?"

"Mr. Prater, go to your truck now."

Mr. Prater's hands clenched into fists. His eyes became wild. "Are you kidding me?"

"Mr. Prater, I am not joking." Ed spoke firmly. "Go to your vehicle now with your boy."

For a moment, Mr. Prater stood there, opening and closing his fists. The three men glared at one another. Finally, Mr. Prater grabbed the back of Prater's shirt and turned with him to leave.

"That's it?" Prater yelled up to his dad. "He gets away with it?"

"Come on," Mr. Prater said gruffly under his breath.

"I can't believe this," Prater shouted as his dad pushed him along to their truck. Prater turned and locked eyes with me. "I hate you! I hate you and your stupid dog."

"Shut up," Mr. Prater said and jerked Prater forward.

Prater wrenched away and faced me again. "You killed mine; I'm going to kill yours. I'll leave poison meat outside for him. I'll set leg traps by the corral. I'll—"

"Get in," Mr. Prater said. He gritted his teeth. Without another look at us, he got in, slammed the truck into reverse, and tore through the side yard around Ed's patrol car. Gravel shot out from under the tires when he hit the driveway. Then they were gone.

Ed turned to Dad. "It's a shame what happened to that horse," he said, shaking his head.

"Yes, it's a shame. But I don't appreciate—" Dad turned to me. "Joshua, go in the house."

I pulled Jack in, closed the door, and pretended to walk to the living room, but I turned and leaned my ear against the crack of the door.

"Bruce is a hothead," Ed said. "As soon as he picked up his car keys I knew where he was going. That boy of his was so insistent."

"Ed, if either of them ever touches my boy or his dog, I will do something about it."

"Well, now, I do need to talk with you about that," Ed said evenly. "This is the second time someone's pointed to your dog for killing their animal. I have to ask you—what was the dog doing outside?"

"Joshua accidentally let him out—they heard a noise in the yard. We were both right behind the dog; he certainly didn't run all the way to Bruce Prater's."

"Are you sure?"

"Look, he didn't come home with blood on his face." Dad's voice rose with irritation. "Something else is going on here. I didn't believe it at first, but now I'm not so sure."

"What are you talking about?"

"My boy says he heard a coyote the other day, and last night he saw it."

"Rich, do you really believe that?" Ed paused. "I've never heard of a coyote showing up around here before."

"I don't know. He said he heard it howling."

A few seconds passed.

"Well," Ed said. "Could be a fox or a wolf. Let me make a few phone calls, see if any other counties are having wolf problems. In the meantime, keep an eye on that dog. People are scared of him." Ed clicked his tongue. "He sure is a strange-looking mutt."

Dad's voice became formal. "He's a Pharaoh hound. And do me a favor," Dad said. "Tell Bruce Prater to stay off my property."

chapter 38

I scrambled away from the kitchen door when I heard Dad and Ed saying their good-byes. I climbed onto the couch and watched as Ed got into his patrol car and drove away.

Dad slammed the door as he came in. "Joshua," he yelled from the kitchen.

I jumped up. My nerves felt all jangly.

He rounded the corner into the living room. "Where's that picture you took last night?"

"Upstairs."

"Go get it," he said. His cheeks were hard and his mouth set in a straight line.

I took the stairs two at a time and flew back down with the picture. I didn't know what was going on, but I wasn't about to question him.

"Here," I said, looking up to him.

He grabbed it. I stood in front of him while he inspected the picture. He shook his head. "I don't see anything."

He handed the picture back to me and raked his fingers through his hair. He began to pace around the room. "This has gotten so out of hand," he muttered. "Ridiculous." He was talking to himself, working something out.

"If I could just get a better picture . . . ," I said.

"No," he said loudly. Then more gently, "No, it's not going to work. They've already decided who to blame." He paced back and forth like a caged-up lion. "What if I hadn't been home? What if Ed hadn't followed him?" He shook his hands in the air.

"But he won't come back now, right?" I said. "You told the policeman."

"I can't go to work worried that people are threatening you." He stopped in his tracks and looked at me. "C'mere," he said.

I stepped closer to him, unsure of what he wanted, when he grabbed me close and hugged me so tight I almost couldn't breathe. My eyes felt wet and my feelings were all mixed up.

Dad let me go and sighed. "I need to know that you're safe."

"I am safe," I said. What was he talking about?

Dad shook his head. "Joshua . . ." His voice trailed off. Then I saw him look at Jack. "I think we need to find a new home for Jack."

My heart bottomed out. "No!" I backed away from him.

"Joshua." Dad's voice was gentle. "I'll start asking around on Monday."

"No!" I yelled. "You know he didn't do it! I heard you tell that policeman."

"It doesn't matter," Dad said, exasperated. "They think he's done all these things. Look, the police have tagged Jack twice now. I can't have any more of this. I'm not going to have Bruce Prater or anyone else banging at my door again." He turned and paced off from me.

"You only care what people think," I yelled. "You don't even care about Jack!"

Dad whipped around. "I can't care about Jack; I care about you. You don't know what angry people are capable of. I'm done with this. I won't take him to the pound—he's too good for that. But I *am* finding him a new home come Monday."

chapter 39

"I hate him," I said to Ray over the phone. I looked through my bedroom window. Dad was washing the car, but his face was still mad. Even from my distance, I could see the dings in the car doors.

After he'd gone outside, I took the phone into my room and closed the door just as Jack squeezed in. Ray had already heard about Shadow and I told him the rest of the story.

"What are you going to do?" Ray asked.

"I don't know," I said. "It would be great if I could just run away with Jack." I turned from the window and focused on Jack, lying comfortably on my bed. Pain stabbed my heart. "It's not fair," I said.

"Maybe the people would let you visit him a lot," Ray offered.

I squeezed the cord with my fist. "No, he's *my* dog."

"I know," Ray said. We were silent for a moment.

"Alan is real messed up. CeeCee's been crying all day." His voice cracked a little.

I didn't know what to say. Prater lost his horse and I was losing Jack. But at least Jack was alive, not torn down by a vicious attacker.

"What are you going to do about Jack?"

I took a deep breath. "I'm going to catch that coyote."

I heard Ray's breath draw up short.

The trash cans stood below my window. Dad had picked up the mess, but shreds of chicken skin stuck to the driveway. "He was here last night, maybe he'll be back."

"Yeah, but how will you prove it if the camera doesn't work out again?"

I'd already thought that one through. "I just need to get closer. I'll go out on the porch and shoot it."

The line fell silent. Then Ray said, "What if he smells you? Shadow didn't stand a chance against that coyote. It's not safe. Maybe you should get your dad."

I laughed meanly at that. "He's the last person who would help me."

"Try again from the window. I just think—"

"It won't work," I said. "I've got to shoot it from the porch." I mangled the cord in my hand. "He won't get away with it tonight."

chapter 40

Dad and I ate the ham supper in silence. He never asked about the chicken leftovers, so I didn't offer any explanations.

Jack lay at my feet under the table. I cut a nice thick, juicy chunk of ham and slipped it to him. He chomped it in a couple of bites and licked his chops until every drop was cleaned off. The ham was delicious, a brown-sugar sauce coating it. Jack liked it; so would a coyote. I sawed off another piece and gave it to Jack.

Dad put his fork down. "That's enough ham for the dog," he said.

"Okay," I mumbled. I didn't meet his eyes.

"Look, I know you're upset about Jack," Dad said. "You probably won't believe this, but I am, too."

I lifted my eyes to Dad.

He leaned both elbows on the table. "This is a sacrifice we have to make so we can live in peace with our neighbors. I promise I'll find a great home for him. I know a couple of guys who have farms—"

"No! I don't want to hear that." I yelled. "It's your fault. We always have to move because of you. I'm tired of making friends and then moving away. Now you want to get rid of Jack."

I scraped my chair back and stood. "All you care about is the stupid air force and your car. I wish you were dead and not Mom." I slammed the chair into the table and stormed up to my room.

I thought he'd pound up the stairs and bang on my door, but he didn't. The house was silent. I strained to hear Jack's nails clicking on the wood. Nothing. The smell of the ham must have kept him under the table. I felt even more alone without him.

My friend Scott had written back to me yesterday. I picked up the envelope and reread the letter:

Hi, Josh,

A family with six girls moved into your house. They play jump rope in the middle of the kickball field. We're getting transferred, but we don't know where yet. Wouldn't it be great if we moved by you?

213

You're lucky to have a dog. At least you have someone you can count on.

Your friend,
Scott

I heard a knock at the door. "Joshua?" Dad called from the other side; then he opened the door. Jack trotted in and leaned against me.

"Hey," Dad said in a gentle voice. "I've got to run to the office for a minute. Want to come?"

I shook my head.

Dad sighed and looked down. "Okay. I'll be back in a little while." He left without closing my door.

I stayed in my room petting Jack until I heard the car back out of the driveway. I cupped Jack's face in my hands. He looked up at me with trusting eyes. Scott was right—I could count on Jack. Now it was time for Jack to count on me.

"I'm not going to let him take you away," I said.

Jack nodded his head out of my hands and licked my palms. I wrapped him in a tight hug, then let him go. I had to reset the trash cans with bait *now*, while Dad was gone. I could not take a chance on Dad catching me out of the house later tonight.

Down in the kitchen, I started to slice up the ham. I felt mad and sad at the same time, and cutting the ham was hard. I put the knife down and tore it apart with my bare hands.

"There you go," I said, throwing a slab to Jack as I backed out of the door with the roasting pan. Jack leaped on his treat and I stole outside.

I could still smell some of the chicken from last night, but I wanted to make sure the bait was strong enough to bring that coyote back. The smell had to be overpowering, irresistible, leaving him no choice but to follow his nose. I smeared the meat all over the cans like I did before, and I let the juice from the pan slurp down the insides of both trash cans. Then I balanced the lids on the tops. Pulling the trash cans out a little bit, I set them in the perfect position to be caught from the window and the porch.

Jack licked my fingers when I went in. My heart turned with sorrow from his easy joy, but I was glad he was happy. He deserved to be happy.

After washing my hands, I got the camera and hid it in the cupboard right by the back door. Everything was ready.

chapter 41

Jack and I settled on the couch. I read a few comic books, lingering on the back pages. Sea monkeys for sale. They had a drawing that showed you the sea monkeys swimming in a fish bowl. They were a regular family, a mom, a dad, a couple of kids. The sea monkeys had faces and you could see they were all happy. It didn't cost too much to get them. Might be kind of cool.

Suddenly I heard the clatter of the trash can lids. Jack barked and jumped off the couch. Still pretty early; must be raccoons. I got up and looked out the window.

Coyote.

My heart hammered wildly. My feet froze in place and my mind went blank. A sharp bark from Jack brought me into focus.

I ran to the kitchen, stumbling over Jack, who ran beside me.

"Stay here," I commanded. I threw open the cupboard and snatched the camera from the shelf, opening the back door at the same time. I started through the door but the strap caught on the doorknob.

"Oh, no," I said, trying to jerk the strap free.

In that moment, Jack squeezed out behind me and bounded down the porch steps.

"Jack!" I yelled. I saw the coyote tear up through the woods with Jack not far behind him.

I dropped the camera and charged out the door after them.

"Jack!" Images of Shadow flashed through my mind, mangled flesh and bone. Mutilated cats and chickens.

The sound of thrashing branches and my pounding footsteps filled my ears. I spotted Jack ahead and flew even faster through the woods. Thin branches whipped my cheeks, but I felt no pain. I focused on Jack's trail, yet I was aware of the entire woods. My thoughts reduced to action: jump, duck, faster.

We ran at a sharp right angle and I began to see through the trees to a clearing. I heard a muffled pop. *Prater's yard.* The coyote slipped out of the woods and bolted across the lawn to the upper wood line. Jack flew out of the woods next and raced across the yard.

As I came out of the trees, I saw Prater coming down the

tree house steps with his rifle. Prater looked up, saw me, then glanced in the direction I was headed and spotted Jack. A look of pure hatred crossed his face. He pulled the lever down, loaded the gun, and ran after Jack.

"No!" I shrieked.

Prater ran fast up the clearing; he had a good head start on me. Fear, deadly fear, washed over me as I watched him disappear into the upper woods after Jack.

A new course of energy flowed through me. My feet became quicker and my movements more sure. I lit through the clearing and sliced into the woods. I could see Prater a short distance ahead of me. Anger fueled my flight.

"Stop!" I shouted.

He didn't break pace. I raced forward, closing the gap between us, so close I could hear his heavy breathing. I reached out and snatched the hem of his shirt. He jerked away and kept running. I fell forward but regained my footing and charged him like a bull after a red flag. He went down with me on top of him. I grabbed the gun and hurled it away with all my might.

Prater scrambled and threw me off, grunting. Then he jumped on me, crushing my ribs with his knee. All the wind got knocked out of me. I looked into his eyes. They were full of hate. Everything he'd done to me this summer flashed by in an instant. I summoned up all that was in me and, roaring, I slammed my fist into his gut.

He groaned and fell to the side, clutching his stomach.

I had no time to waste on him. I tore up the mountain following the direction I'd last seen Jack.

"Hey!" Prater's angry voice called up to me. I glanced back. He'd grabbed the gun and was trying to catch up.

I set my face forward. I was not afraid. This mountain was mine and Jack's territory.

I reached the top of a small hill and stopped. My chest heaved and my lungs were on fire. My heart beat fast but strong, and I held my breath for a second. Then I heard a kind of huffing sound, like Jack and I had heard before. I followed the sound up the tree line and crept around a dense thicket.

There, in front of a huge overturned tree, stood the coyote. Jack was not ten feet from it.

We stood in a deadly triangle.

The coyote looked like a wiry German shepherd, gray with black mixed in. He lowered his stance and held his bushy tail straight out from his back. His lips curled back to reveal sharp, white teeth. His yellow eyes shifted from Jack to me.

The hairs on the back of my neck stood up. My chest hollowed out with fear. My legs locked and I couldn't move my arms.

I looked at Jack. He stood erect, with his skinny tail curved over his back. Fur bristled along his spine. He knew I was there, but he didn't waver—his eyes were set on the coyote.

Heavy footsteps plodded around the bushes. "Now you're going to get it," Prater shouted. "You and your stupid dog—"

His words hung in the air; his footsteps froze behind me.

The coyote rumbled a wicked growl.

"Shoot." My voice came out as a croak. "Shoot!"

I turned. Prater stood like a white statue. He was stupefied.

"Gimme the gun!" I grabbed it out of his useless hands and in the same motion cocked it and turned back to see the white underbelly of the coyote lunging at me. I roared and fired the gun, but not before I saw Jack leap toward the coyote.

He was power and grace, his fur golden as he jumped through the last rays of the sunset. His eyes blazed with purpose. His ears flushed with heat. His body arced like an arrow through the air, each flank showing hard muscle. He was beautiful.

I saw a flash of teeth, heard the report of the rifle, and both Jack and the coyote fell to the ground. The coyote did not move again.

My legs gave way and I sank to the ground. I dropped the gun. I was dimly aware of Prater moving around now behind me.

"Jack, Jack," I murmured, crawling up to him. "It's okay," I said gently. But when I cradled his head, I saw that it was not okay. That it would never be okay. Jack's throat was ripped open. Blood colored his neck and spilled onto the dirt.

My shoulders shook and tears filled my eyes, spilling over. I pressed my lips together to hold back the hurt, but I could not stop the tears that rolled down my cheeks. "Jack . . .

Jack . . ." A painful ache welled up in my throat. With one hand, I swiped at my eyes.

Jack jerked his back legs, trying to get up. I let out a yelp racked with pain and sorrow. Jack's eyes were wet and the rims of his eyes faded. His ears paled. Tears blurred my vision of him.

I looked up at Prater, who was still white. "Help me," I said hoarsely. "Please!"

chapter 42

Prater bent down and stared, mouth open. He was still in shock. I pulled off my shirt. Piecing Jack's skin back, I wound the jersey around Jack's neck. Then I carried Jack like a baby in my arms down the mountain, Prater at my side.

"I'm sorry," he said. He started mumbling; he was breaking down. But then I remembered it was only this morning the coyote killed his horse.

"Just help me," I said and he nodded in return.

When we broke through the trees to his yard, Prater ran ahead, yelling. His dad stomped out onto the porch, already angry at whatever it was. His face changed after Prater shouted a few words to him. He ran around the side of the house, hauled up in his truck, and lurched to a stop beside me.

"Get in!" he yelled, throwing open the passenger door.

Prater helped me with Jack and plopped on the seat beside me, slamming the door shut. Mr. Prater wheeled the truck around and sped through town, past Puchalski's, past my street, past Ray's house and Tysko's. I would have gone back in time to any of those places just to change tonight.

Streetlights lit up Jack's face in flashes.

Please, God, please, I prayed.

Mr. Prater jerked the truck to a stop in front of the veterinarian's office.

"Stay here!" he yelled and jumped out. He ran to a small house behind the office and banged on the door. A porch light came on. I heard Mr. Prater's voice, charged with urgency. Both men ran back to the truck.

"Let's get Jack into my office," Dr. Hart said. His face was concerned and his voice gentle. He tried to take Jack.

I shook my head. "I'll carry him."

Dr. Hart nodded and ushered us into his office.

After I laid Jack on the table, Dr. Hart took over. He spoke to Mr. Prater and I heard him, I heard his voice, but the words didn't make any sense.

Finally he looked at me and said, "Why don't you boys wait in the other room?"

I shook my head.

Mr. Prater stepped forward. "Boys," he said, then turned to me. "Let's go call your dad."

I fastened my eyes on Jack. The white sheet under him was now streaked with blood. Jack's eyes and ears were pale, his lips almost white. I touched his head. "I'll be back," I said to him, fighting off tears.

In the waiting room, I collapsed on the couch. Mr. Prater called Dad. My arms were smeared with Jack's blood. My chest was stained brownish red. I leaned my head back against the wall and closed my eyes. I heard Prater and his dad murmuring, but I couldn't pull myself up. My body was too heavy and the dark room pressed in on me.

Suddenly a car crunched through the gravel outside and screeched to a stop. I opened my eyes. Dad burst inside, his face wild. He took one look at me and his voice cracked.

"Joshua." It came out as a sob. He covered the room in a few steps and crushed me to him. "Joshua, Joshua, Joshua." He rocked me on the couch.

My chest shuddered as I fought back my own tears.

After a while, Dr. Hart came out. I jumped to my feet. His white coat was flecked with blood.

"Well?" Mr. Prater said.

Dr. Hart glanced at him and then turned to me. "Fifteen stitches. He'll probably have a scar."

"A scar? You mean he's okay?" My eyes watered and my heart leaped. "Jack's okay?" I shouted. Dr. Hart nodded and I heard him talk about rabies and antibiotics and keeping him overnight, but I couldn't concentrate—my heart and soul were too busy celebrating.

"I want to see him," I interrupted. Without waiting, I burst through the door to the treatment room.

Jack's neck was shaved and golden stitches laced his skin together. Blankets and hot water bottles surrounded him. He lay still on a rug in the corner.

I knelt on the ground beside him and lightly stroked the top of his head. He opened his eyes and without moving his head, he looked at me. His lips and ears were still pale, but his amber eyes radiated strength and life, and I saw for my own self that God had answered my prayer.

Dad walked in and crouched beside me. "This dog's a hero," he said, his voice husky. He put his arm around my shoulders. "So are you."

I didn't want him to think I was crying, so I looked down before any tears slipped out.

He squeezed my shoulders. "If Dr. Hart says it's okay, Jack's coming home with us tomorrow. To stay."

chapter 43

J ack looked real good in the newspaper picture of us they put on the front page. His stitches were in plain sight, but I saw them as a badge of courage, like how the reporter described it.

The paper quoted wildlife officials saying coyotes lived all over Pennsylvania but sightings were rare. Coyotes had pups in the late spring and were more aggressive about getting food for their litters, especially if the food was easy prey, like penned-up chickens or other small livestock. Get an electric fence and don't leave your pets outside, the article said.

The pastor did a big sermon on me and Jack, saying there is no greater love than to lay your own life down for another. He made me stand up and everyone clapped.

We brought Jack home after church. Millie came by and

gave me a big hug. "I almost fainted when I heard the news," she said, dabbing her eyes with a tissue. She pulled a great big bone out of her bag and laid it beside Jack, who was nestled in a corner of the kitchen. He sniffed it but laid his head back down. His neck was way too sore to wrestle with a bone that big just yet.

Then the phone started ringing and people kept running up the porch and banging on the door to see me and Jack. Ray came, more newspaper people, Ed, Pastor Danny, Mark, our neighbors. They kept saying how brave I was and what a good dog Jack was. I worried about Jack with all that commotion, but people mainly wanted to lay their eyes on the dog who took down the coyote, and he was rightly deserving of their admiration.

Some kids whose faces I recognized showed up.

"Were you scared?" one kid asked.

"Yeah, what was it like?"

I thought about Jack leaping up to save me, me firing the gun. I thought about that coyote who hunted only to survive. I shook my head. "I don't feel like talking about it," I said.

They egged one another on with their own versions of what happened. Wonder and awe filled their eyes. I was too tired to even correct them. And I decided not to tell anyone why Prater had really been up the mountain.

After a while, I had to take a break from all those people. I crashed on the living room couch and closed my eyes. A loud rapping at the door startled me, but when I answered it, no one was there. Then I saw a little box on the porch. I stepped out, opened the box, and found in it a golden strap of leather. The figure of a dog had been etched into it.

I stared at it for a second, rubbing my thumb over the cut leather. Someone else might not have noticed the care he'd taken to give the ears just the right point or the noble, almost graceful, lines he'd carved for Jack's body. An image of Prater laboring over this figure flashed in my mind. I snapped the band onto my wrist and turned back into the house.

Millie had laid out chips and little sandwiches and pink lemonade. I didn't know where it all came from, but the whole thing turned into kind of a party, with people streaming in and out of the house all day long. Finally, it grew dark and Millie closed the door after the last well-wisher, tidied up, and went home herself.

Dad locked up after her. "Boy, some day, huh?" he said.

I nodded. I was beat.

Dad turned off the lights and motioned me upstairs.

I shook my head. "I'm sleeping down here," I said. Jack's neck was purpled with bruises. I didn't want him trying to get upstairs like that.

Dad brought down a sleeping bag and my pillow, and after a few words, he went upstairs to bed. I got a flashlight and aimed it at the ceiling.

Lying next to Jack on the floor, I could just make out his

face. He licked my hand. I traced the star on his snout. His fur was like velvet and his eyes precious amber jewels.

Jack laid his head down and closed his eyes. I stroked his back gently. His breath was soft, easy. *Sweet Prince William.*

I leaned over and turned off the light.

acknowledgments

This story is close to my heart, and I'm happy to have the opportunity to thank the people who helped me bring it to life. I thank God for giving me the gift and inspiration to write; my agent, Ted Malawer, who believed in this story from the beginning; Loren and Sue Sherod, who shared their Vietnam-era experiences with me, Loren as an enlisted man, and Sue as the girl who waited for him back home. Risa Saltman generously gave me an entire afternoon, a cup of coffee, and her memories of those tumultuous times. I'd also like to acknowledge Jack Saltman, who served in Vietnam and never let Neil or Pam have toy guns.

My father was an air force recruiter toward the end of the Vietnam War (though it was never officially declared a "war"). My dad always had a joke for you, a new card trick, or a good candy bar. I never knew about the things that had

acknowledgments

happened to him while he was a recruiter until I was an adult and he shared some of his experiences with me. When he first started reading my work, he told me, "If I could do this, write like this, I wouldn't do anything else." I think he would be proud of me and of this book.

Maria Madgett supports me with her friendship and prayers. Matthew Haworth dazzles me every day with complex yo-yo tricks, hence Ray's love of yo-yos. Michelle Carr and Steve Haworth read countless versions of the manuscript and took the time to offer thoughtful comments and suggestions. My sweet brother Chris, who no longer walks this earth, came over every day for a week, put on the ugly reading glasses, and read the manuscript out loud with me until we were both hoarse and laughing too much. He loved Joshua and Jack, but he really hoped I would follow up with a story called *Prater*.

My editor, Stacy Cantor Abrams, makes me a better writer. I am grateful for Stacy and all the people at Walker who work with me to give the reader the best experience possible— getting lost in a book.